Charmed Life

Mia's Golden Bird

Charmed Life

It's Raining Cupcakes

Sprinkles and Secrets

Frosting and Friendship

Charmed Life

Mia's Golden Bird

LISA SCHROEDER

SCHOLASTIC INC.

ISBN 978-0-545-60377-5

12 11 10 9 8 7 6 5 4 3 2 1   14 15 16 17 18 19/0

Printed in the U.S.A.   40
First printing, June 2014

For my birding friends, Margie and Dolores

Chapter 1

American Robin
every summer, baby birds fly from the nest

A box had arrived in the mail for Mia.

Not just any old box, but a box from one of Mia's best friends, Caitlin, whom she'd met at summer camp a few months ago.

Mia's hands shook with excitement as she opened the box. Inside she found a large baggie of homemade cookies, a letter, and something small wrapped in tissue paper. Her heartbeat quickened. She slowly peeled back the tissue, wondering if it might be the one thing she was really hoping for.

When she saw the charm bracelet, Mia let out a little squeal. Caitlin had chosen her to wear it next! She pulled the bracelet out of the paper completely and whispered, "Awesome," as she fingered the cute flower charm Caitlin had picked out. The bracelet no longer looked sad and lonely, the way it had the last time she saw it at camp. *Like a dog without a bone,* Hannah had said.

The thought made Mia smile.

She fastened it on her wrist and just like every other time one of the Cabin 7 girls had put on the bracelet, a camp memory came to mind.

In Mia's memory, the four girls, Mia, Caitlin, Libby, and Hannah, had just gotten back from a trail ride. It was the first time Mia had ever been on a horse, and she'd enjoyed it up until the point where her horse, Jet, had stepped on a wasps' nest in the ground and gotten stung. All Mia had known at that point was that Jet flew off the trail and through the woods, giving his name new meaning. Mia had held on tightly, but when she had to duck to avoid a low branch, she lost her balance and fell to the ground with a loud *thud.*

She was okay, thankfully. But the barn wasn't exactly close by, so she'd had to get back on the horse and continue to ride the trail. Mia's three friends had been so kind and caring once they'd finally reached the end of the ride.

"Are you terribly sore?" Libby had asked her with her sweet British accent. "Shall we carry you to the cabin?"

Hannah, her southern friend, had given Libby a funny look. "Carry her? What is she, a sack of potatoes?"

Caitlin had stepped in and said, "Here, Mia. Put your arm around my shoulder and lean on me. Hannah, you're closest to Mia's size, get on the other side of her and do the same."

Mia had started to resist but changed her mind. They'd really wanted to help her, and so she had let them. Once they were back at the cabin, her friends had insisted she rest on her bunk until dinnertime. The next day, the soreness really hit. Fortunately, the camp nurse gave her ibuprofen, and it had helped with the pain over the next couple of days.

Now, Mia sighed. It was so nice to have a strong memory of camp, even if it wasn't her most favorite one because of the silly fall. She missed Camp Brookridge. More than anything, she missed her friends. Especially right now, when all of her friends at home were busy doing things Mia couldn't do. She looked down at the walking cast she wore and stuck her tongue out at the stupid thing. No soccer. No surfing. No nothing, it seemed like. How ridiculous that she'd fallen off a horse and managed to not break anything and yet, when she fell off a simple step stool at the café a couple of weeks ago, she'd landed funny and fractured a bone in her foot.

As she nibbled on a cookie that tasted like cinnamon, she

read Caitlin's letter. She smiled, reading about how Caitlin had wanted to send a fruit pizza — which the girls had fallen in love with at camp — to cheer Mia up. It would have been too messy though, so she'd sent cookies instead. Caitlin wrote about making new friends and being in the school play with them.

It was good to hear that Caitlin seemed happy after a rough start at her new school. When Mia got to the part in the letter about the bracelet, she forced herself to read it slowly.

I hope you enjoy wearing the bracelet and the flower charm. Pretty flowers are like my Cabin 7 BFFs — they brighten up my life so much.

I know you're dying to know if the bracelet is lucky. I think you'll have to find out for yourself. I can say this: I feel super lucky to have so many great friends, and you are one of them.

Be happy! Remember, sometimes _awesome_ shows up when you least expect it. I know it's your favorite word, so I hope you get a whole bunch of awesome real soon!

Love,
Caitlin

So Mia would get no clue at all as to whether the bracelet was really lucky. Oh well. She actually felt better than she had in weeks, simply by wearing it, so that was something.

She stuffed the cookies back in the box, grabbed her camera, and went out to the kitchen. Her mom sat at the kitchen table with a bunch of paperwork in front of her and looking a little frazzled, her long black hair piled high on her head in a messy bun.

"Look, *Mamá*. Caitlin, one of my camp friends, sent me cookies. Do you want one?"

"How nice," her mother replied. "*Sí*. I'd love to try one."

Mia put a few cookies on a plate, poured some milk for the two of them, and sat down across from her mom who was studying a piece of paper in front of her.

"You don't look very happy," Mia said as she picked up her glass of milk. "Everything okay?"

Her mother nibbled on a cookie. "Mmm. *Delicioso*." She looked at Mia. "Paying bills is not very fun. Times like these, I really miss your father. It's much easier to have someone to share the responsibilities with."

Mia nodded, although she couldn't really understand what it was like for her mom. Not really. It had been just the

5

two of them for as long as she could remember. Her father, who had been a marine, went to Afghanistan shortly after Mia was born. He never came home. She was only four years old when she had attended his funeral.

"I thought the café was doing well," Mia said, taking another cookie.

"Fairly well," her mom said. "The cost of supplies has gone up though. And the tourist season will start to wind down now. It's always a bit harder in the winter." Her mother shook her head. "*Todo está bien*. I shouldn't talk about this with you, Mia. I don't want you to worry."

"No, it's all right," Mia said. "I don't mind. And I want you to know I'm going to find a way to help pay for camp again next summer. I don't know how yet, exactly, but hopefully something will come up."

"We need another set of twins born in the neighborhood," her mother teased.

Last spring, Mia had helped their neighbor, Mrs. McNair, every afternoon after school. Mrs. McNair had given birth to twins and already had two older children to care for. Mia went over and played with the older children or helped with laundry or whatever else Mrs. McNair needed until her husband, a professor at a nearby university, got home from work.

"A mother's helper" was what Mrs. McNair had called the position. She'd paid her well, and Mia had used all of her money to pay for more than half of the camp fees.

She worked for her mother at the café sometimes too, usually on the weekends, but that money was put into a savings account for college.

"I'll figure it out," Mia said, her insides twisting into a knot as she thought about it. What if she didn't come up with a way to make some money? What if she had to stay home next summer, while the rest of her cabin friends returned without her?

Her mother interrupted her anxious thoughts by reaching out and touching the bracelet on Mia's wrist.

"*Muy bonito*. Did your friend send that along as well?"

Mia nodded. "I know, it's beautiful, isn't it? The four of us bought it in a fun little shop during our field trip at camp. We're taking turns wearing it."

Her mother stood up. "That is sweet. Good friends are a treasure. We must always remember that. Now, I'm going to make us some dinner." She pointed to the camera. "Are you going to the beach?"

"Just for a little while, if that's okay."

Her mother nodded. "You've been off your foot for most

of the day, so I suppose a little walk is fine. Take it easy though. And please be back in thirty minutes."

Mia kissed her mother on the cheek and then hobbled to the front door, her camera in hand. Maybe she couldn't get in the ocean, but at least she could still look at it.

Chapter 2

Seagull
they will eat almost anything

It was a beautiful fall day — warm and sunny with a slight breeze. It reminded Mia how, at camp, Caitlin had asked if it was true what they said about Southern California and its perfect weather. Mia had told her it was absolutely true. Though it was also true that Southern California had some of the worst traffic anywhere. That fact didn't affect Mia much, however, since she could walk to the beach from her house. She thought about how thankful she was to be able to do just that as she slowly made her way down the sidewalk and toward the access trail.

Mia had probably been to the beach near the small cottage where she lived more than a thousand times over the years. She never grew tired of it. Never grew tired of searching the sand for shells and special rocks or taking photos of the sea and the sky and trying to capture the beauty as she looked out at the horizon. It was only recently that her mother finally let Mia come here alone, with her camera and cell phone. She wouldn't ever be allowed to surf alone, of course. Too dangerous. But wandering the beach by herself to take photos or whatever was something Mia had begged to do for a long time.

Because it was just the two of them living in the cottage, Mia sometimes felt smothered. It'd been hard for her mom to let Mia go off to camp all the way across the country, to New Hampshire, but Mia never gave up, and finally, her mom had agreed. It was often a tug-of-war between the two of them, her mother wanting to keep Mia close and safe and Mia seeking independence any way she could get it.

The soft sand was hard for Mia to walk in with her walking cast, so she made her way closer to the water, where the sand was firm from the waves hitting it over and over again. Once there, she searched the sand for treasures, her thoughts still focused on her mother, who had worked so hard all of these years to support the two of them. She was thankful for everything her mom did for her. It could have been much worse, and she knew that. Still, sometimes she couldn't help but be envious of her friends, who had it a lot easier than she did in the money department. Worrying about finances and whether she could get to camp again next year was about as much fun as wearing a walking cast.

Up ahead, Mia saw a couple of her friends, Salina and Josie. They waved, and she waved back. Mia took her camera and snapped a photo of them walking toward her, the ocean on one side of them and the sandy beach on the other.

Salina was one of the prettiest girls in sixth grade. Tall, dark, and lean, with one of the nicest smiles Mia had ever seen, Mia had always thought her friend could become a model, if she wanted to. Of course, Salina always laughed it off when someone told her that. Salina was a straight-A student and dreamed of medical school someday. Josie was strong and athletic, like Mia. And she was funny. The three girls had been friends for a long time. So long, that Mia couldn't even remember a time when they weren't a part of her life.

When Salina and Josie reached her, Mia asked, "Hey. What are you guys up to?"

"We're heading up to Gill's," Salina said. Gill's, a diner by the beach that had been around forever, was known far and wide for their fresh strawberry shakes and their sweet potato fries. Just the thought of fries and a milk shake made Mia's stomach rumble.

"A bunch of us from the team are meeting there for dinner," Josie told her. "You know, to celebrate our win this morning. Aren't you coming?"

Mia shook her head. "No. Nobody told me."

"You left so fast after the game, we probably didn't have a chance," Josie said. "Where'd you go, anyway? Your mom take you out for your favorite breakfast, pigs in a bunk bed?"

This was a running joke with the girls. Every time they saw "pigs in a bunk bed" on the menu of their favorite breakfast place, they laughed about it. The first time, it had been Josie who'd said, "I can just see little pigs, lying on bunk beds, covered in pancakes to keep them warm." The dish was delicious yet simple — sausages nestled within the layers of pancakes.

Mia smiled as she replied, "Nope. No pigs in a bunk bed for me. My mom had to get to work. Anyway, it was a great game. You guys were really awesome. Not that I need to tell you that."

Now Josie smiled. "Thanks. We were pretty awesome, weren't we?" She held her hand up to Salina and they high-fived.

Mia waited for her friends to say they missed having her on the field with them. Or that it would have been even more awesome if she'd been playing. Something. Anything that let her know she was still an important part of the team, even if she couldn't exactly be a part of the team right now. At least, not in the way that it mattered. But they didn't say anything.

"Well," Mia said softly, "guess I should let you guys go. Don't want you to be late or whatever."

"You can come if you want," Salina said, tucking her thick, wavy hair behind her ears. "It's no big deal."

Mia didn't like feeling as if she were a second thought. If they hadn't run into her, would they have even missed having her there? She imagined everyone sharing stories about the game and talking about plays she hadn't been involved in. She wouldn't have a thing to say, really. On the other hand: a milk shake and sweet potato fries. Not to mention a chance to hang out with her friends, which she hadn't done much lately.

As she glanced down, weighing the pros and cons of the situation, her eyes landed on the stupid cast. She'd have to hobble along beside them, all the way to Gill's.

"Thanks, but I can't," she said, looking back up at her

friends. "My mom's making dinner right now. I should probably get home. You guys have fun though. And have a strawberry shake for me."

Was that relief she saw on their faces? Mia wondered.

"Okay," Josie said. "See ya later."

"Yeah. Later."

As the two girls continued down the beach, Mia started to take another picture but changed her mind. Her pictures were supposed to cheer her up, not depress her. And watching them walk away without her, to have fun with the team, celebrating a win Mia hadn't really been a part of, definitely would not cheer her up.

When she got home, her mom told her to get a plate and dish up. She'd made rice and beans and heated up some tamales from the batch she'd cooked yesterday. Mia sat quietly, eating, while her mom talked about an article she'd just read about how a couple of cups of coffee a day are good for you. Because of the café, coffee always seemed to be on her mother's mind.

After dinner, Mia went to her room and flipped through her CD collection. This is what she did when she was feeling down, because dancing in her room, by herself, always made her feel better. She went back and forth, trying to decide between a boy band from Australia called Underground Bliss, and her favorite actor/singer from the Whimzy channel, Levi Vincent.

She decided to go with Levi Vincent. She loved his voice *so* much. And man, was he cute.

As she started to move and groove, the weight of her cast was noticeable once again. Not only that, her foot was starting to hurt a little bit, after walking to and from the beach. She tried to ignore it. Tried to tell herself it didn't matter, that she could stand still and dance.

But it just wasn't the same.

She plopped down on her bed with a big sigh, the charm bracelet poking her hand as she landed on it.

"You need to bring me some luck," Mia whispered, fingering the pretty flower charm. "Soon. Really, really soon."

Chapter 3

Parrot
extremely recognizable

$\mathcal{S}$ix out of seven days, Mia's mom had someone else open the café early in the morning. This allowed her to see Mia off to school during the week and attend activities like soccer games on Saturday mornings. But Sunday mornings, both Mia and her mother woke up early so they could open the café by six.

It hadn't always been this way. The café used to be closed on Sundays, but her mom finally decided she couldn't miss out on the revenue a second weekend day would bring, especially during tourist season.

So for the past few years, it had become part of Mia's weekly routine. She worked side by side with her mother, serving customers or helping to bake muffins in the back. But when Mia got her walking cast, the doctor had told Mia she should be careful to not overdo it and to stay off the foot as much as possible. Her mother had insisted this meant no more working at the café until the cast came off. Mia still wanted to go along with her mom though, just in case it got busy and she needed her. She didn't tell her mom this, of course. Instead, Mia told her she liked the coziness of the café and it was as good of a place as any to put her feet up and read or do homework. This particular Sunday, she decided she wanted to work on putting together a scrapbook of camp photos.

Earlier in the week, Mia and her mom had visited the craft store where Mia was allowed to pick out a scrapbook along with some special glue, pens, and stickers. Now, she grabbed the bag containing all of those supplies, plus the envelopes of photos she'd had developed at the drugstore. She also brought her camera along, because she believed a true photographer should always be ready, just in case a good photographic moment presented itself.

The café wasn't far from their cottage, but since Mia had broken her foot, they drove instead of walked. As they pulled into a parking spot across the street, Mia said, "*Mamá*, just so you know, I'll probably never get on that step stool again. Anything up high is all yours."

Her mother laughed. "Still mad about your accident?"

"Furious."

"Your cast will be off before you know it," her mother said as she reached over and touched Mia's cheek. *"Ten paciencia."*

"But how can I possibly be patient? My friends are all off having fun without me. It feels like I've had this stupid thing on my leg for a hundred years already. And I still have twenty-three miserable days left. It's not fair."

"This isn't like you, Mia."

"What do you mean?"

"This negative attitude of yours. I don't like it. Maybe your scrapbook will bring you some joy today, yes?"

Mia sighed. "I hope so." She looked at her mom. "I'm sorry. It's just . . . hard, you know?"

"I know. Come on. Let's go inside and I'll make you a cup of hot chocolate and get you a muffin."

It wasn't long until the smell of brewing coffee filled the café. Mia's mother had told Mia she could start drinking coffee occasionally when she entered middle school if she wanted to, but Mia had discovered she didn't care much for the taste. The smell, however, she had come to love.

Mia sat at a table near the window, flipping through photos and sipping her drink from a big white mug. This particular stack of pictures contained the ones from their last few days at camp. The all-day hike with a picnic half-way through. The final campfire and awards ceremony. And breakfast on the last day, before everyone headed home. It made Mia both happy and sad all at the same time, remembering the fun she'd had with her friends and thinking about how life hadn't been fun at all since she'd broken her foot. It also made her even more anxious to find a way to make some money so she could go back next summer.

Customers trickled in and out, and Mia mostly ignored them. Until a girl with blond hair piled back in a messy twist and wearing gold-rimmed sunglasses peered over her shoulder.

"Ooh, cool pictures. Where were those taken?" she asked Mia.

"Camp Brookridge, in New Hampshire."

"Like, a sleepaway camp?" the girl asked.

"Yep."

"Ohmygosh, how fun! I would kill to be able to go to something like that."

"Lacy, dear," an older woman said. She wore khaki clothes and a brown safari hat. She looked like she was ready for some kind of adventure. "What kind of latte did you want again? I can't remember."

"Pumpkin spice, if they have it," she said.

"Yep. We have it," Mia told her. "It'll go away in December though, when we bring out peppermint."

Mia studied this girl named Lacy. Why did she look so familiar? Mia was positive she didn't go to her school. Had she come in here before, maybe?

"Wait," Lacy said to Mia. "Do you, like, work here?"

"Sometimes," Mia replied. "My mom owns it."

"Oh. I see."

Mia waited for the girl to leave. To walk over and join Ms. Adventurer. But she stood there, staring at the pictures scattered all over the table.

"Can I ask you something?" Lacy asked.

Mia shrugged. "Sure."

"I know this is probably going to sound strange, but, I'm wondering if maybe you'd come along with me and my grandma Gail and take some pictures for us."

Mia stared at the girl. Of all the things she might have thought the girl would ask, this was definitely not one of them.

"Uh. Well. What kind of pictures, exactly?"

"Don't laugh."

"Okay."

"Grandma Gail is a big bird-watcher. I go along with her sometimes because it's so quiet and peaceful when we're looking for birds. It's one of the few times I feel normal, you know?"

Mia nodded even though she didn't understand at all. What kind of girl would feel "normal" when she was out with a woman wearing a safari hat, looking for birds?

"I could pay you," Lacy said. "Whatever you think is fair for a few hours of your time."

"I don't know," Mia said. "I mean, I'm not a professional. I'm just a girl who likes taking pictures."

Lacy reached up, pushed her sunglasses onto her head, and looked sternly at Mia. "Please don't ever say that. If you want to be a professional, you can be a professional. Whether you're a kid or not, it doesn't matter. Look at me. I'm both a kid and a professional, right?" She smiled. "Sorry. Didn't mean to go all mean girl on you. I just get a little annoyed when people don't give themselves enough credit."

Mia tried to take in what Lacy was saying, but she was having a hard time. Now that Mia could see Lacy's entire face, she knew exactly why she recognized this girl.

She was Lacy Bell.

As in, the movie star Lacy Bell.

Chapter 4

Great Crested Flycatcher
the female works hard to build the Nest

$\mathcal{L}$acy was one of the most well-known teen actresses in Hollywood. She'd started out as a kid, with her own TV show on the Whimzy channel. Mia had grown up watching the show. Then, last summer, Lacy had been in a movie called *Mystical Creatures*, about two sisters who discover a family of unicorns in the woods by their house. Mia had gone to see it with some of her friends.

They'd liked the movie, but they hadn't been especially fond of Lacy Bell being in the film. Lacy had become one of those actresses who people talked badly about, because it seemed like she was everywhere now. Like, she had just come out with a collection of perfume along with a line of sunglasses. And she'd been cast in two more movies coming out in the next couple of years.

"Here you go, dear," Lacy's grandmother said, coming up to Mia's table. Lacy turned and took the pumpkin spice latte from her grandmother's hand.

"Grandma, I've asked..." Lacy looked at Mia. "Ohmygosh, I'm so sorry, I didn't even get your name."

"Mia," she said. "Mia Cruz."

"I've asked Mia if she would go along with us and take pictures. I want to make a scrapbook like she's doing. Isn't it fabulous?"

"Yes," her grandma said, her eyes crinkling at the corners as she smiled. "Wonderful. Marvelous. A splendid idea, Lacy. Three sets of eyes will certainly be better than two, as we continue our search for the seemingly shy light-footed clapper rail."

"That's one of Grandma Gail's life birds," Lacy explained, like it made perfect sense.

Except it didn't make any sense to Mia, so she raised her eyebrows and replied, "Oh-kay."

Lacy laughed. "Don't worry. We'll get you up to speed on what you need to know in the bird department. Do you need to ask your mom for her permission? She'll let you go, won't she?"

Mia was frozen in place. She didn't know what to do.

Going off to look for birds with these two, um, interesting people did not exactly sound like a good time. On the other hand, Lacy had offered to pay Mia. And obviously, based on Lacy's occupation, she could definitely afford it.

"Yeah, let me go talk to her," Mia said as she stood up. "I'll be right back."

Lacy's mouth dropped open when she saw Mia's cast. "Oh no. Are you okay to walk around? It doesn't hurt, does it?"

"It's fine," Mia said. "It's a walking cast, specifically so I can walk around. I mean, I have to be careful. Take things slow. But yeah, if you're planning on walking miles and miles, then I'm definitely not the photographer for you."

Lacy looked at her grandmother. "It's okay, right? We don't have to go very far today. And maybe we can sit on one of the benches along the trail for a while and watch for birds that way?"

"Perfectly fine," she assured the girls. "Now go ask your mother so we can get going. You know what they say. The early bird gets the worm."

Mia found her mom in the back, pulling some muffins out of the oven. The delicious aroma told her they were banana, one of the more popular flavors. Unlike other cafés,

Coffee Break served only muffins alongside the menu of hot and cold drinks. It made it simpler for Mia's mom. She bought mixes that required just milk and eggs, so making them didn't take a whole lot of work.

"*Mamá*, you aren't going to believe this, but I've just been offered a job."

Her mother took off the oven mitts and placed them on the counter. "Really? What kind of job?"

"Taking pictures of birds."

"Who wants you to do that?"

Mia went closer and whispered. "Do you know who that is, in our café, right this very minute? It's Lacy Bell. You know, from *The Lacy Bell Show* on the Whimzy channel that used to be super popular? She's in movies now, but you know who she is, right?"

"Of course I do. Who's the woman with her?"

"It's her grandma. Her name is Gail."

Mia's mother crossed her arms. "So I'm supposed to trust two complete strangers because one of them is a movie star?"

There she was, Mia's overprotective mother, making an appearance again. "Well," Mia said patiently, "she *is* one of the most famous actresses in the entire country. Can you imagine if something happened while I was with her? Her reputation would be ruined forever. Besides, it's bird watching, not skydiving. I'll be fine."

Her mother narrowed her eyes. "But, Mia, what about your foot? You're supposed to take it easy."

"And I will. There are benches at the place where we're going. *Mamá*, please. I'm guessing she'll pay me really well."

Her mother sighed. "Let me go talk to the woman and see if there's a way to put my mind at ease." She reached out and touched Mia's cheek. "You can't blame me for wanting to keep my one and only *hija* safe."

Mia stayed back, watching through the crack of the swinging doors, while her mom talked to Gail and Lacy. After a few words were spoken, Gail reached into the small purse she carried, took out a wallet, and handed it to Mia's mother. Mrs. Cruz took a peek at the ID inside the wallet and then shook Gail's hand.

"They seem very nice," she told her daughter when she returned to the back room. "I've decided you can go. I have her wallet and will keep it until they return you, safe and sound. But keep your cell phone on and call or text me if there's anything that makes you feel uneasy. *¿Entiendes?*"

"Yes, I understand. I'll be fine." Mia kissed her mother on the cheek. "Thank you for letting me go. I'll see you in a few hours."

"Are we ready?" Gail asked when Mia returned.

"Almost," Mia replied as she quickly cleaned up her scrapbook stuff. After she set everything behind the counter, out of the way, she grabbed her camera and with as much enthusiasm as she could muster she said, "Okay. Let's do this."

"Great!" Lacy said. "We are going to have so much fun. You'll see."

And with that, Lacy put her sunglasses back on, and in true movie-star fashion, walked to the door with long, confident strides. She stepped through and held it open for Mia, who shuffled out and stopped dead in her tracks when she saw what was waiting for them.

A shiny black stretch limo.

Chapter 5

Black-capped Chickadee
curious about everything

"Sorry," Lacy said. "I know it's flashy and so cliché, but my mom needed the town car today. I hope you don't mind."

Mia didn't know how she felt, honestly. It was like she'd stepped out of the café and into some strange alternate reality.

Is this really happening? She blinked a couple of times, because, obviously, it was happening, and she needed to act like all of this was completely normal.

"Oh yeah, it's fine. I don't mind," Mia said, trying to play it cool.

"Wonderful," Gail said. "Then let's shake a tail feather and get going, what do you say?"

The driver opened the door and Mia got in first. She took a seat, and Lacy sat down next to her, even though there was lots of room and she could have sat anywhere. Mia scooted over a little bit, to give them both some space.

Once Gail got in and sat across from the girls, the car started moving and Mia asked, "So, where are we going?"

"Batiquitos Lagoon," Gail told her. "It's a birder's paradise — a great combination of vegetation and geology that attracts waterfowl, shore birds, birds of prey, and perching birds. Have you heard of it, dear?"

"Yes," Mia said. "But I've never been there."

"It's beautiful," Lacy said. "Great trails to explore." She looked at Mia's cast. "But don't worry. We won't walk much, I promise."

Mia watched as Lacy took off her sunglasses and put them in her neon green purse. Then she took out a compact, opened it up, and powdered her nose and cheeks. Mia suddenly felt self-conscious. The only makeup she ever wore was lip gloss, and she didn't even have any of that on today. In fact, she'd barely brushed her hair that morning before she pulled it back quickly into a ponytail.

"I'm curious," Mia said. "Is there a reason you're going so early?"

"You know what they say," Gail said with a wink. "The early bird —"

Lacy interrupted her. "She's just being silly. That's not the real reason. If you honestly want to know, it's because we can leave the house without any paparazzi following us if we get up at the crack of dawn on a Sunday. They follow me practically everywhere these days, but Sunday mornings they're either going to church or sleeping in, I'm not sure exactly. All I know is that Sunday mornings are about my only chance for a little freedom."

Mia had so many questions she wanted to ask Lacy. She wasn't sure how old she was, but she was pretty sure she was only a little bit older than Mia. Where did she go to school? Or were Hollywood actresses given a free pass when it came to school? Did she live in Hollywood or somewhere near by? And most important, why in the world did she choose to spend her one free morning, when she could probably do whatever she wanted, bird-watching with her grandma?

"Can I ask you something?" Lacy said. Mia wanted to reply, *Only if I can ask* you *something*. Or a bunch of somethings.

But instead she said, "Sure."

"What'd you do to your leg? Or foot, or whatever?"

Of all the things Lacy could ask, she had to ask about *that*. Mia sighed. "I fell off a step stool at the café. It was really stupid. I have a hairline fracture in one of the bones of my foot. The worst part is that I can't surf with my friends, or play soccer. I'm out for the rest of the season."

Lacy's eyes got big and round. "You play soccer? Oh, wow. I've never met a soccer player before. What's that like?"

Mia bit her lip, trying not to laugh. She'd never met anyone who played soccer? Was she serious?

"Well, I think it's awesome. But, it's a lot of running, and making a goal is a lot harder than it looks, you know?"

"Do you play with boys and girls or just girls?" she asked.

"Just girls."

"Are you good friends with most of them?" Lacy asked.

"I guess so," Mia said, trying to forget about not being invited to Gill's yesterday.

"Bird watching's our sport, right, Lacy dear?" Gail said. "Remember, birds of a feather must flock together."

Lacy stared out the window. "I guess so."

"So what's a life bird?" Mia asked.

Lacy seemed to be lost in her own thoughts, but Gail said, "Most birders have a life list, which is a list of special birds they dream of seeing at least once during their lifetime." She reached down into a canvas bag and pulled out two notebooks, a black one and a purple one. "Lacy and I both keep track of the birds we've seen as well as the birds we hope to see one day."

"Does that mean that some birds are harder to find than others?" Mia asked.

Gail nodded. "Most definitely. Some birds are on the endangered list, due to their decreasing population, which makes them more difficult to find. And then some are simply good at hiding, like the clapper rail. It's a very, very secretive bird and rarely comes out of the marshes. But the search is part of the fun, right, Lacy?"

"Yes," she said.

Searching for birds didn't sound like much fun to Mia, but she wasn't coming along to judge them, she was coming to take pictures for them.

Lacy was quiet the rest of the way, so Mia stayed quiet too. When they pulled into a parking lot a while later, Gail grabbed the bag that held the journals and both she and Lacy tucked their purses underneath the seat. "I don't even take my phone with me when we're out here," Lacy told Mia. "It's truly an escape. For a little while, anyway."

The driver opened the door and Lacy stepped out first, then Mia, and finally Gail.

"Does the driver just wait for you?" Mia asked.

"Yep. That's his job. To drive me around wherever I need to go. And he does spend a lot of time waiting too. But he's a big reader, so he always has a book with him. He likes murder mysteries." Lacy shuddered. "I don't get that at all. I hate scary books and movies."

Mia nodded. "Same here."

Gail handed Lacy a pair of binoculars with a long strap, which she slipped around her neck. "This way, ladies," she said, walking toward a trailhead.

"What would you like me to photograph, exactly?" Mia asked. "The two of you, or the birds we see, or . . ."

"Anything and everything," Lacy said. "I just want lots and lots of pictures so I can make a scrapbook like you were making back at the café."

Anything and everything? This was going to be the easiest photography job ever, then. She let Gail and Lacy walk ahead and she started taking pictures. After they'd walked a little ways, Gail turned around and put her finger to her lips, telling Mia to be extra quiet. Lacy pointed up ahead, where a couple of birds darted through the air and over the path. Mia tried to get a picture, but they were gone before she had the chance. Maybe this wasn't going to be so easy after all.

Mia caught up to them and asked, "What kind were those?"

"Say's phoebes," Gail replied. "They're quite common here in California. They catch insects midair."

Lacy made a mark in her notebook, and then they continued walking.

"So, are you from Mexico?" Lacy asked Mia.

Mia resisted the urge to roll her eyes. "No."

"But you are Mexican, right?"

"I'm a lot of things," Mia said. "Mexican, Guatemalan, white. I have a white grandfather."

"So if you're not Mexican, what are you?"

Mia wanted to say *human*. Instead, she simply replied, "Latina."

"Is it just you and your mom?" Lacy asked.

This interrogation about Mia's life was kind of irritating, but she didn't know how to tell a big movie star that she was being rude. Mia decided to change the subject. "Shouldn't we be quiet so we have a better chance of seeing more birds?"

"Sorry," Lacy said. "I'm just curious about you, that's all."

Before Mia could figure out how to respond to that, Gail pointed to a spot in the distance where two little birds pranced around on the ground. Lacy grabbed her binoculars while Mia went to work trying to get a picture.

Hopefully, there would be a lot more birds that would keep Lacy's attention, because Mia found it very strange to have a movie star so curious about the life of an ordinary sixth-grade girl.

Chapter 6

California Condor
the Size might Surprise you

$\mathcal{B}$ack in the limo a couple of hours later, Gail and Lacy were discussing some of the birds they had seen. Unfortunately, the light-footed clapper rail was not on the list of birds they'd found that morning.

"Hope is the thing with feathers," Gail said, her brown eyes practically twinkling as she said it. "We must remember, there's always next time. What was your favorite, Mia? If you don't mind my asking."

"I loved seeing that flock of white pelicans," Mia told her. And she meant it. Bird watching had ended up being a lot more fun than she'd thought it would be. "Oh, and the osprey was pretty cool too. I got some really nice shots that I think you'll like a lot."

"Wonderful," Gail replied with the same easygoing smile

she wore most of the time. She seemed like a genuinely nice person. "Fantastic. Makes me happy as a lark. What about you, Lacy?"

"I'm so excited to see the photos," Lacy replied. "How long will it take you to get them developed, Mia?"

"If I take the memory card to the drugstore tomorrow after school, I should have them back by Wednesday."

Lacy nodded but didn't reply, like she was thinking about something. Mia decided it was her turn to ask some questions. "So, do you go to, like, a regular school?"

"No," Lacy said. "I wish, but no. Because of my work schedule, I have tutors. They come to the set with me, and we'll do work during the downtimes."

"Sounds pretty good to me," Mia said. "No boring classes that way. Or teachers who talk about anything, whether it's important or not, because they have an automatic audience."

"But school is about so much more than classes, you know?" Lacy asked, playing with the pretty gold-and-diamond ring in the shape of a bow that she wore on her right hand. "It's about friends and cute boys and making fun plans for the weekend. I don't get any of that. Sometimes I think about missing prom in a few years, and I get so sad."

"How old are you?"

"My mother likes to say thirteen going on twenty-three. I guess that means I'm mature for my age. All I know is it feels like I'm missing out on everything that's fun about being a teenager."

Mia didn't know what to say. Finally, she said, "I'm pretty sure there are a lot of people who would love to trade places with you."

"Oh, I know. It probably sounds like I'm complaining, and I don't mean to, it's just . . ."

"The grass is always greener on the other side, isn't it?" Gail said. "I do believe it's quite normal to long for things we don't have."

Was Mia supposed to feel sorry for Lacy? Is that what she wanted? Because there was no way that would ever happen. Mia thought of her mom, struggling all of these years to make sure they had food and clothes and a roof over their heads. It seemed like the only thing Lacy had to worry about was whether she should take the town car or the limousine if she wanted to go somewhere.

What a problem to have, Mia thought.

The girls were silent the rest of the way back. Mia was glad. It was pretty obvious the two girls didn't have much in common, so it was better this way. Easier.

When they finally pulled up in front of the café, Mia said, "When do you want to come and pick up the pictures?"

Lacy reached into her cute designer purse, pulled out a wallet, and opened it up. What happened next about knocked Mia over.

The actress held out a hundred-dollar bill. "Is this a fair amount?"

"But, you haven't even seen the pictures yet," Mia said. "What if they're terrible?"

Lacy laughed. "Ohmygosh, they're not going to be terrible. I'm sure they're wonderful. Look, I saw the ones you took at your camp, and if they're anything like that, I know I'm going to love them. Besides, your time is worth something, right? Go on, take it."

Mia reached out and took the money. Was this really happening? A hundred dollars, for just a few hours of her time?

"I really appreciate you coming along with us," Lacy said. "And if you're up for it, I'd love for you to join us next Sunday too. That way, I can just pick up the pictures then."

"Next Sunday?" Mia asked. "You mean, you want to do this again? With me?"

"Yes," Lacy said with a smile. "Why wouldn't we? Right, Grandma?"

"Most certainly. Definitely. Absolutely," Gail replied. "We'll be proud as peacocks to have you accompany us as our photographer, young lady."

Mia looked down at the money she now held in her hand. She'd never even seen a hundred-dollar bill before, let alone held one. It was nice and crisp. New-looking. As if Lacy had recently gotten it from the bank, fresh out of the vault, or wherever it was that money came from.

Maybe Lacy had been kind of nosy at first, and a bit insensitive about the questions she asked. And maybe she was clueless about how good she really had it. But she wasn't a horrible person. And her grandma was very sweet.

Besides all of that, it was a dream job for Mia. Ten times easier than playing with little kids. No gross little noses to wipe, no messes to clean up, and no whining to deal with. Sure, Lacy had complained a little bit. But she hadn't whined for hours on end, which had happened a few times with Mrs. McNair's kids. And the benches at the lagoon made it an ideal place to sit and watch for birds, so she didn't have to be on her feet very much at all.

"Okay," Mia said. "I'll go with you next week. Will you pick me up at the same time? Here, at the café?"

"Yep," Gail said. "Because you know what they say."

"The early bird gets the worm?" Mia said.

Gail smiled. "Actually, I was going to say, 'Without coffee, life's not worth living,' which is why we'll happily pick you up at the café again."

Just when she thought she had Gail all figured out, Mia thought, smiling back at the older woman. Apparently, Lacy's grandmother *did* think about other things besides birds once in a while.

"Okay," Mia said. "I guess I'll be going now. See you next week."

"Grandma, don't forget your wallet," Lacy said.

"Oh, yes, of course," she said. "I'll escort you inside, Mia."

"'Bye," Lacy said. "And thank you *so* much. Really and truly."

When Mia and Gail stepped inside the café, Mia's mom was at the counter. She greeted them with a smile and said, "Oh, good. You're back. Did you have fun?"

"We sure did," Gail said. "Absolutely terrific. Your daughter is a true delight."

Mia's mom handed Gail the wallet. "I think so too," she said.

"I'm going again next Sunday morning," Mia told her mother. "I hope that's okay?"

"More birds to see?" Mia's mom asked Gail.

"Always," she said. "And more fun to be had with my granddaughter."

Mia had to admit, the love Gail showed for her granddaughter was pretty wonderful. Gail was one unique bird. The thought tickled Mia. All that bird talk had obviously rubbed off on her.

Chapter 7

Screech owl makes ghostly sounds in the night

At school on Monday, Mia wasn't sure whether to tell people about her adventure with the famous actress. What would her friends think about that? Would they be impressed, or would they think it was ridiculous? She couldn't be sure, since some of them thought Lacy herself was kind of ridiculous. Which, now that Mia thought about it, didn't really seem fair. They didn't even know her.

Mia found Salina, her locker partner, at their locker, talking to Josie along with *her* locker partner, Polly.

"So what time should we meet up?" Salina was asking.

"The waves are best in the morning," Polly said. "That's what my dad says anyway. And he said Sunday morning is best for him. And since we need to have an adult with us . . ."

"What are you guys talking about?" Mia asked as she

took off her backpack and unzipped it to get to the books inside.

"Surfing," Josie replied. "This coming Sunday. My dad surprised me with a new board yesterday. He found it at a garage sale super cheap, and it's in really good condition. Can you believe that?"

"You're so lucky," Polly said, reaching back and pulling her blond ponytail tight.

"I wonder if someone died and that's why it was for sale," Josie said. "And what if he haunts me while I'm out on the waves? Like that weird story a while back about the surfers who said they saw a girl's face a few feet below the water as they surfed? One girl even said a hand reached up and grabbed her ankle. It tried to pull her into the water, but luckily, she shook it loose." Josie held up her hands and wiggled her fingers and said, "Ooooh," in a spooky voice. "Surfing ghosts are so scary."

Salina laughed. "Was that in one of those weird newspaper magazines they have at the grocery store checkout stand? You know, the ones where everything inside is basically *made up*?"

"What?" Josie said. "No way. Surfing ghosts are totally real. Right, Mia? Back me up on this one."

Mia had moved over to the open locker, where she quietly put her books away and gathered the items she needed for first period.

"I've never seen one," Mia said, the heaviness in her chest returning as she thought of her friends, off having fun without her. Again. "But then, I also haven't been surfing in a while."

"Maybe that's a good thing," Josie teased. "No surfing ghosts are gonna get you."

Mia turned around, trying to smile. "I guess so."

Salina put her arm around Mia. "Sorry you can't surf with us. You can come and watch us if you want."

"Bring along some garlic," Josie said. "Chase those ghosts away for us."

"That's for vampires, silly, not ghosts," Polly said, laughing. "And stop it with the ghost thing. There are no surfing ghosts. Nothing but little, harmless fish out in that ocean with us, right, Mia? And yes, you can come and watch us if you want to. We'll try to give you a good show."

"I can't," Mia said. "I already have plans. I mean, I have a new job."

Everyone's eyes got big and round as they turned and stared at Mia. "What kind of job?" Salina asked. "And how come you're just now telling us?"

"Maybe because you were too busy talking about scary surfing ghosts," Mia replied.

"So spill," Josie said. "What are you doing?"

Mia held her books to her chest as she said, "I'm working for Lacy Bell. She came into the café yesterday and she asked me to help her with something. She said she'd pay me. And so I said yes. And I'm doing it again next Sunday too."

The girls looked at Mia as if she had just told them surfing ghosts were about to invade the school.

"Lacy Bell?" Salina said. "As in, the actress Lacy Bell?"

"Yes," Mia said. "The one and only."

"What exactly are you doing for her?" Polly asked.

"Well, I'm taking photos. I'm, like, her personal photographer for the day."

"You're kidding," Josie said, crossing her arms across her chest. "Right? This is some kind of joke, isn't it?"

Mia shook her head. "No. It really happened. Honest."

"What do you take pictures of?" Polly asked.

Mia hesitated. She didn't want to tell them about the bird watching. It might sound kind of strange to them. They probably would doubt her even more if she gave that as her answer.

"She wants to make a scrapbook of the time she spends

with her grandmother, so we just go out and walk around, and I take pictures."

"That's it?" Josie asked. "Just . . . take random pictures? Like she couldn't do that herself with her camera phone?"

"Not if she wants really good, quality photos," Mia explained, trying not to get upset. Why couldn't they just be happy for her?

"Huh," Salina said. "So, what's she like?"

Mia shrugged. "She's okay. Kind of . . . clueless about some things. But that makes sense, you know? She lives such a different life compared to most girls. Like, she doesn't go to school. Tutors go to the set with her."

"Well, that sounds rough," Josie said. "Poor little rich girl."

Before Mia could respond, the bell rang. The girls finished gathering their things for class and then took off together, down the hall. Once again, Mia trailed behind everyone, as she shuffled along because of her cast.

"You'll have to get some good gossip on her, Mia," Polly said, turning around as she said it. "Then report back. Maybe we can sell a story to a magazine and get a lot of money."

"Yeah," Josie said. "Maybe the magazine that reported on the surfer ghosts would be interested."

The three girls laughed. Mia kind of felt sick to her stomach. She never should have told them about Lacy Bell. To them, it was all a joke.

To Mia, it was a real job. A way to get to camp. And that wasn't funny at all.

Chapter 8

Bald Eagle
a bird you'll find in lots of books

After school, Mia went to her room with a couple of Caitlin's cookies and a glass of milk. She sat down at her little desk and pulled out a piece of paper and a pen.

DEAR CAITLIN,

THANKS FOR YOUR LETTER AND FOR THE DELICIOUS COOKIES. I'M EATING THE COOKIES RIGHT NOW, SO IF THERE ARE A FEW CRUMBS IN THE ENVELOPE, YOU'LL KNOW WHY. I CAN'T BELIEVE YOU FIGURED OUT HOW TO MAKE A FRUIT PIZZA. DID IT TASTE JUST LIKE THE ONE WE HAD AT CAMP? WHERE'D YOU FIND A RECIPE, ON THE INTERNET OR SOMETHING? YOUR SISTER IS SO LUCKY!

ALSO, THANK YOU FOR SENDING ME THE BRACELET TO WEAR NEXT!! I LOVE THE CHARM YOU PICKED OUT.

I'M HAPPY YOU'VE MADE SOME FRIENDS AT YOUR NEW SCHOOL AND THINGS ARE BETTER FOR YOU NOW. THINGS ARE ABOUT THE SAME HERE, WHICH MEANS MY FRIENDS ARE STILL OFF HAVING FUN WITHOUT ME AND I'M STILL FEELING JEALOUS. I'M TRYING SO HARD NOT TO LET IT BOTHER ME, BUT IT DOES. THEY ACT LIKE THEY DON'T EVEN CARE IF I'M WITH THEM OR NOT. IT'S ABOUT THE WORST FEELING IN THE WORLD, FEELING LIKE I COULD JUST DISAPPEAR FROM THE FACE OF THE EARTH AND NONE OF THEM WOULD HARDLY NOTICE.

SOMETHING KIND OF INTERESTING HAPPENED YESTERDAY THOUGH. DO YOU KNOW LACY BELL, THE ACTRESS? WELL, SHE CAME INTO MY MOM'S CAFÉ AND ASKED ME TO GO BIRD-WATCHING WITH HER AND HER GRANDMA AND TAKE PHOTOS FOR THEM. SHE SAID SHE WOULD PAY ME TO GO WITH THEM. SO I SAID YES. WE SAW SOME AMAZING BIRDS.

DO YOU THINK BIRD WATCHING IS WEIRD? I WASN'T SURE WHAT I THOUGHT, BUT IT ENDED UP BEING KIND OF COOL. THERE ARE SO MANY DIFFERENT KINDS OF BIRDS. I DON'T THINK I EVEN REALIZED HOW MANY. I PROBABLY STILL DON'T REALIZE HOW MANY. ANYWAY, I'M DOING IT AGAIN NEXT SUNDAY. BUT I'M AFRAID TO TELL MY FRIENDS

ALL OF THIS. THEY KNOW THE PART ABOUT LACY BELL BUT NOT ABOUT THE BIRDS — THEY THINK LACY IS RIDICULOUS, SO I DON'T KNOW WHAT THEY'D SAY ABOUT THE REST OF IT!

WELL, I GUESS I SHOULD FINISH THIS UP AND GET GOING ON MY HOMEWORK. GOOD LUCK WITH THE PLAY. OH, WAIT. THAT SHOULD BE BREAK A LEG. THEATER TALK FOR GOOD LUCK, RIGHT?

I MISS YOU!

YOUR CABIN 7 BFF,

MIA

She found Caitlin's address in her camp journal, put the letter into an envelope, and sealed it up. If only she could deliver it in person, she thought. Wouldn't that be awesome, if she could just teleport to Connecticut really fast, give Caitlin a hug along with the letter, and then come back home? Of course, it wouldn't be so easy to leave once she was there. She'd probably end up staying and sleeping on Caitlin's couch forever, so they could make fruit pizza together every night.

When Mia got up to grab her books out of her backpack, she glanced at her surfboard, sitting in the corner. She went over to it and ran her hand down the smooth fiberglass. No one knew it, but she had a nickname for her board. She called it Nemo, because the orange and yellow colors reminded her of the fish in one her favorite movies.

"Do you miss the water as much as I do?" she asked Nemo.

She shook her head as she plopped down on the floor. "Great," she whispered. "This cast is making me so crazy, I'm now talking to my board like it's a person."

In her mind, she could see herself out on the ocean, paddling on her board toward the waves. She could almost feel the sun on her face and the cold water running through her hands. But most of all, she could feel her legs, free and light, with no cast to weigh her down.

She put her head in her hands and groaned. *Why did this have to be so hard?* Mia wondered. She decided she needed to keep her mind off surfing. Most likely, her friends would be talking about their upcoming fun day of surfing all week long. She had to find something that she could be excited about. And what was the one and only thing she had coming up that was something other than school, homework, and sleeping?

Bird watching.

She needed to get excited about bird watching. How she

might do that, she wasn't sure. But she decided maybe a good place to start would be the library. So tomorrow at lunch, while her friends talked nonstop about hitting the waves on Sunday, Mia would go and check out some books.

She gave Nemo one last pat and whispered, "Sorry."

If it could talk, she was pretty sure it would have said, *It's okay, Mia. Hang loose.* Because Nemo was awesome like that.

Chapter 9

COMMON LOON
listen for its lonely cry in the evening

At lunch the next day, Mia scarfed down a peanut butter and jelly sandwich and a few chips in about three minutes and then stood up from the table.

"Where are you going?" Josie asked.

"I, uh, need to go to the library and do some research," Mia said, crumpling up her paper sack.

"For what class?" Salina asked.

"Not for class," Mia said. "Something for my mom. Sorry, I gotta go. See you guys later."

They probably thought it was strange, but she didn't want to tell them what she was doing. Besides, now they could sit and talk about surfing and soccer all they wanted and didn't have to worry about Mia feeling left out. Not that they seemed to worry about that very much anyway.

When she got to the library, the librarian, Mrs. Lennon, said, "Hey, Mia. How's it going?"

"Okay, I guess," she said. "I was wondering if you have any books on birds or bird watching?"

"I think I remember ordering a couple of books that might fit the bill," Mrs. Lennon replied. She typed something on her computer keyboard. "Let me check and see if they're in." She glanced up at Mia, shifting her eyes just above her reading glasses, which sat low on her nose. "Are you taking up a new hobby?"

"Well, I've met some people who like to go bird-watching, and I want to learn more about it," Mia told her. "I'm actually going along with them and taking pictures."

"Mia, that sounds wonderful."

"Do you really think so?" Mia asked. "You don't think it's . . . weird?"

Mrs. Lennon laughed. "You have to remember, I'm a librarian. Any time a student tells me about a new learning opportunity, I'm going to think it's a good thing."

Mia smiled. "Yeah, I guess you're right. I wish I could know for sure whether my friends would think the same thing."

"My aunt is a bird-watcher," Mrs. Lennon said. "I've gone with her a few times. It's fun!" She pulled out a piece of paper and wrote something down. "I know it's hard, but try not to worry about what other people think. If you like it, that's all that matters."

"I guess," Mia said softly. "I just don't want them to make fun of me."

"I know," Mrs. Lennon said. "I think the key is to make sure they know how important it is to you. If they care about you, and they know it's important to you, they should support you. Be understanding about it, right? That's what good friends do for each other."

Mia nodded. When she said it like that, it made perfect sense.

Mrs. Lennon reached her hand out, holding the piece of paper. "Here are the numbers you want to look for in the nonfiction section. Do you remember how the Dewey decimal system works from the talk I gave the first week of school?"

"I think so," Mia said.

"Well, let me know if you need help," she said.

Mia found the books fairly easily and checked them out. "I hope you enjoy them," Mrs. Lennon said.

"Thanks," Mia replied.

She rushed to her locker, hoping to get there before

Salina so she could stick the books in her backpack in privacy. But it didn't work out that way.

"What books did you get?" Salina asked, stepping aside so Mia could get in to the locker.

There was no getting out of it now. Mia held them out so Salina could see them. "Birds?" she asked. "Your mom is interested in birds?"

Mia shrugged. "What's wrong with birds?"

"Nothing," she said quickly. "I just . . . it wasn't what I was expecting, that's all."

Mia thought about what Mrs. Lennon had said. She should probably be honest and tell Salina the books were really for her. But then Salina would probably start talking about Lacy Bell again, and she didn't want to talk about her.

Mia sighed as she put the library books into her backpack so she wouldn't forget to take them home.

"Is everything okay?" Salina asked. "You're acting kind of different. To be honest, you've been acting different for a while."

Mia turned around, a wave of anger washing over her. "You mean, since I broke my foot, I've been acting different? Well, I bet you would be too, if all your friends were going off, having fun without you, doing things you can't do."

Salina bit her lip and didn't say anything for a few seconds. It was obvious she was trying to figure out how to reply. Finally, Salina narrowed her eyes and said, "I'm sorry, Mia. I'm sorry if you feel left out. But what do you want us to do, sit around and feel sorry for you? That's all you seem to want to do."

As soon as the words hit Mia, she could feel her eyes and nose tingling, like the tears were going to start falling any moment. She turned around, grabbed the books she needed for her next class, and slammed the locker door.

"Thanks a lot," Mia muttered as she walked away, not as quickly as she would have liked because of the stupid cast. She headed for the bathroom, where she could cry in peace until the bell rang.

Chapter 10

Apostle bird
Native to Australia and travels in groups

What do you want us to do, sit around and feel sorry for you?

The words Salina had said after lunch played on repeat in Mia's brain for the rest of the afternoon. On the bus ride home, she tried to tune them out by putting on her earphones and listening to some music, but it didn't work very well.

How could one of her very best friends say that?

Mia fingered the charm bracelet, thinking about her best friends from camp. None of them would ever say something like that. Would they? Then she remembered what her mom had said on Sunday. *This negative attitude of yours. I don't like it.*

Didn't her friends here at home understand how hard

it was for Mia to have to sit on the sidelines? What was she supposed to do, pretend she was happy when she wasn't?

If only she were an actress, like Lacy Bell. Maybe she could just act her way through life. But the more Mia thought about it, the more she wondered if maybe the words had been hard to hear because they were kind of . . . true.

What was she going to do about it, was the question. So she couldn't do her favorite things for a while. It wasn't like her foot would be in a cast *forever*. It was temporary. In the meantime, one amazing thing had happened to her, and she needed to focus on that. She had a job to earn money for camp. Not just any job, but a job that allowed her to do one of her favorite things — take photos.

Mia made up her mind then and there to not let her broken foot get her down anymore. There were plenty of other things to be happy about, including the letter from Hannah that she found waiting for her on the kitchen counter when she got home.

Her mom, who closed the café every day at three so she could be home with Mia after school, greeted Mia with a snack of apple slices and string cheese.

"How was school today?" her mom asked.

"I checked out a couple of books about birds and bird watching from the library," Mia said as she pulled off a string of cheese. "I want to learn more about it before Sunday. Oh, and that reminds me, I need to go to the drugstore and get this week's photos developed. Can you take me when I'm finished with my snack?"

Her mom looked at the clock. "Give me about fifteen minutes, and I'll be happy to take you. I need to make a phone call first."

"Okay, thanks," Mia said.

Her mom took the phone into her bedroom and shut the door. Mia opened the envelope and started reading Hannah's letter.

Dear Mia,

Your poor foot!!! Oh my goodness, I feel so bad for you. Does it hurt? I bet you're missing soccer and surfing something fierce.

Somehow, you have to look on the bright side. Let's see, what would the bright side be? I know, you could learn how to do something new, something you've always been interested in.

Like, you could learn to knit or crochet. My grandma crochets beautiful hats and baby blankets. Does that interest you? Oh, wait, you probably don't have much of a need for hats or sweaters or blankets in Southern California, do you?

What about cake decorating? I've always thought it would be so fun to learn how to do that. Except that requires you to be standing in the kitchen a lot, and maybe you don't want to be standing too much.

I know! You could learn to play an instrument, like the piano or guitar or violin or something. I could see you playing the guitar. What do you think?

There must be something you'd like to learn more about. You know how much I love animals, I'd probably be using some of the downtime as a way to learn more about animals I don't know much about. Like koalas, for instance. I know they're cute and they live in Australia, but that's really all I know. Maybe you can go to the library and check out some books on subjects you've always wondered about. While your leg gets better, your brain will get bigger. Your mama would probably love that, right?

Nothing much to tell you about things around here.

Maybe in my next letter. Mostly I just wanted to write to tell you I was thinking about you and hope your foot heals up real nice and things are back to normal for you soon.

Your Cabin 7 BFF,

Hannah

Mia couldn't believe that Hannah had suggested she should learn more about animals after she had just checked out two books about birds. What were the chances? It made her miss her camp friends even more, and she realized she felt closer to them at the moment than the friends she'd known forever at home. She'd have to write Hannah back and tell her about her bird-watching adventures. Of all people, Mia knew Hannah would be excited and would think it was a fun opportunity.

The more Mia thought about it, the more thankful she felt that Lacy and Gail had invited her to join them on their bird-watching adventures. It was like a special gift sent along by the universe just for her.

She looked down at her charm bracelet. It really was lucky, Mia thought. No doubt about it.

Chapter 11

Magpie
wears lovely clothes

The rest of the week crawled by at a snail's pace. Mia had apologized to Salina for the way she'd been acting, and Salina had said she was sorry for what she'd said, but things still felt different between them. Strained. Mia didn't like it, but she didn't really know what to do about it either. So she just kind of kept her distance and spent a lot of time in the library, reading the books she'd checked out.

Mia was thankful when Sunday finally arrived. Maybe she couldn't go surfing with the rest of her friends and play on the beach all day, but she could take pictures and get paid for it. Hopefully Camp Brookridge wouldn't be just a one-time thing for Mia. After all, she wanted it to be an every-year thing. Until the four girls were too old and couldn't go any-more, of course. What they'd do after that, who knew.

Maybe they'd travel the world together. That could be fun. Or maybe they'd all attend the same college and be roommates. That would be awesome!

She told herself to stop worrying about the future and focus on the here and now. When Mia and her mom got to the café Sunday morning, her mom gave Mia a muffin and some hot chocolate for breakfast while they waited for Gail and Lacy to arrive.

"Could you put two muffins in a bag for them?" Mia asked her mom. "Like, a little gift from us to them?"

Her mother did as she asked and handed the white bag across the counter to Mia. "*Gracias, Mamá*. Not just for the muffins, but for letting me go with them again."

"*De nada, mi hija*. I hope you three have a nice time."

Just then, Lacy and Gail strutted through the front door like a couple of colorful peacocks.

"Good morning to you fine ladies," Gail said, tipping her safari hat toward the two of them. She had on the exact same outfit as last time.

"Good morning," Mia and her mother said together.

Lacy took off her sunglasses and beamed at the three of them. She wore white pants with some adorable red flip-flops and a red-and-yellow tank top. In her hand was a bright yellow clutch. It was kind of funny, how different Lacy and her grandma dressed for bird watching. Gail looked like a professional, while Lacy looked like she was going to a museum or something.

Mia looked down at the shorts and T-shirt she wore, basically her uniform outfit, and realized maybe she should have thought about her clothes a little bit more this time. Compared to Lacy, she looked kind of pathetic. At least she'd taken a shower and made sure her hair looked halfway decent today.

Lacy gave a little wave. "Hi, Mia! I'm so happy to see you again," she said as she walked over and gave Mia a little hug. Lacy smelled like spicy vanilla. It seemed strange to Mia to be hugging when they hardly knew each other, so she just patted Lacy's back a few times before Lacy stepped back.

"May I order some coffee to get this lovely day off on the right foot?" Gail asked Mia's mom.

"Certainly," she replied. "What may I get you?"

"I have muffins for you too," Mia said, holding up the white bag.

"Wonderful," Gail said. "Splendid. Lacy, what would like to drink?"

"I think I'll take a caramel macchiato this time," she replied.

While Mia's mom took their order, Lacy chatted away

with Mia. "I've been so excited about today. I told Grandma one of the smartest things I've ever done was invite you to go along with us last week."

"Oh, well, thanks," Mia said. "Do you want to see the photos I took from last time?"

Lacy squealed. "Ohmygosh, I can't wait."

The girls took a seat at a table, and Mia placed the envelope of photos in front of Lacy. She opened it up and started flipping through the photos.

"Oooh, I love this one," she said, showing Mia a photo of the white pelicans. It was one of the best ones she'd taken that day. Two pelicans stood back-to-back, and their long, colorful beaks really stood out.

Lacy continued looking until her grandma came over and handed Lacy her drink. "Grandma, wait until you see these. They are fabulous."

Gail looked at Mia and winked, something she seemed to enjoy doing quite a bit. "Of course they are. Just like the girl who took them."

Lacy put the photos back into the envelope and stuck it in her purse. Then she stood up with her drink in her hand and said, "Okay. Let's get this show on the road, as my mother likes to say."

Mia grabbed her camera bag and the muffins, and they headed outside, where a much simpler car, though still very nice, waited for them. The town car, Mia assumed. The driver opened the door for the girls, who climbed into the back while Gail got into the passenger seat in front.

"So, how was your week at school?" Lacy asked as they began driving down the road.

"Not too great," Mia admitted.

"Oh no," Lacy said. "How come?"

Mia stared out the window. She remembered how she'd promised to not feel sorry for herself anymore. This was her chance to show the new Mia in action. She turned and looked back at Lacy. "You know, forget I said that. It was fine. Just kind of . . . long. I'm glad the weekend is here."

Lacy leaned her head back against the seat. "Oh, me too. I had two twelve-hour days on the set. One of the other actors kept forgetting his lines. It was miserable."

"I don't know how you do it," Mia said. "Memorizing all of your lines, I mean. Isn't it hard?"

"I guess sometimes it is, but I don't really think about it. It's what I have to do, so I just do it. I read them over and over, out loud sometimes, because that really helps." Lacy smiled. "Isn't it strange? To you, memorizing lines seems hard, and to me, I can't imagine being able to get up on a surfboard and stay there through the crashing waves. Like, it just seems impossible."

Gail turned around and asked, "Mia, I'd love to have that muffin you brought along, if you don't mind."

"Oh, sure. Sorry, I forgot." Mia passed her the bag, so Gail could take hers out, and then Gail passed it back to Lacy. She set the bag down beside her.

"I'll save mine for later, if that's okay. I had some toast before we left."

"Does your grandma live with you?" Mia asked.

"Kind of," Lacy replied. Mia looked at her curiously. "She has a little house on our property. That way she has her own space, but we're nearby. I see her just about every day. Sometimes in the evening she comes up to the house and we watch that TV show where they visit different farms and follow the people around to see what it's like. She grew up on a farm, so she loves that show. Gosh, I can't think of the name of it right now. Do you know what it's called?"

Mia's eyes lit up. "Yes! It's called *Heart of the Farmer*. I love that show too!"

Lacy laughed. "You do? I thought we were the only people who watched it. I don't know why it's so fascinating to me."

"It seems like such a simple and hard life, all at the same time," Mia said. "Sometimes I think I'd love it, and other times I think I'd hate it."

"Exactly," Lacy said. "Me too. You know how you went to summer camp last year?"

Mia nodded.

Lacy fiddled with her ring. "I thought about going to this camp where everyone lives like pioneers. You make quilts, learn about canning, and cook things like stews and corn bread. Oh, and you have to do laundry the old-fashioned way, with a washboard. Plus, the whole time, you wear pioneer clothes and bonnets."

"Seriously?" Mia asked.

"Doesn't it sound amazing?" Lacy said.

"How come you didn't go?" Mia asked.

"Mostly because of work," Lacy said. She sounded so sad about it, Mia felt bad for her.

"You must miss out on a lot of stuff I don't even think about," Mia said.

"And it's not just because I'm busy all the time," Lacy said. "I don't like to go because it's not much fun being swarmed by people or being followed everywhere I go by the paparazzi. I can't even remember the last time I went to the movies. Or shopping at the mall."

"When do you go shopping then?"

"My manager arranges it so I can go to a boutique and have the place to myself."

"Wow, that must be awesome," Mia said, trying to imagine what that would be like, having racks and racks of clothes all to yourself.

Lacy looked out the window. "Awesome? No, not really. It's pretty lonely, actually."

Chapter 12

Laysan Albatross Sleeps while flying

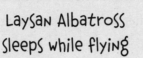

"Would you look at that," Gail said as she and the two girls watched a bird hover over the water like a helicopter for a moment before tucking in its wings and diving like a small rocket into the water and coming out holding a fish in its beak.

Lacy peered through her binoculars as she said, "Oh, wow. I love it. That's a belted kingfisher, right, Grandma?"

"You got that right, sweetheart," she said. "Not a large bird, really, but quite spectacular in its own right."

"That was amazing," Mia said as she scrolled through the camera shots she'd managed to get. One was quite impressive: she had captured the bird flying away from the water, the fish sticking out of its beak. She told herself to look up the gray-and-white bird when she got home so she could learn a little more about it.

A little while later, they saw a snowy egret along the shoreline. The completely white heron with a bright yellow beak and bright yellow feet was stunning.

"He looks so fashionable, doesn't he?" Lacy whispered.

Mia nodded her head in agreement as she took photo after photo until he finally flew away.

"Ah, to be able to do that," Lacy said as she stood up from the bench they'd been sitting on. "To just fly away whenever you want." She looked at Mia, her blue eyes happy and sad all at the same time. "Can you imagine?"

As Mia hobbled along with her clunky cast, she really *couldn't* imagine what it must be like to fly so gracefully and go wherever you wanted. Mia realized both she and Lacy probably envied that about the birds — their freedom and their ability to go wherever they wanted to go. Sixteen more days until Mia wouldn't feel so limited in what she could do. But for Lacy, there really wasn't an end in sight.

Suddenly, it all made sense. That's why Lacy loved to come here. Not only did she feel free for a little while herself, but she also got to watch the fascinating birds enjoying their freedom too. It was kind of like the farming television show they both liked. Maybe they couldn't live like that, but it was fun to imagine what it would be like.

Although they failed to see a clapper rail once again, they did see a snowy plover, which seemed to make Gail happy. It was a cute little bird with a white belly and brown and black markings on its back and head.

"They're on the list of endangered birds," Lacy explained to Mia. "Anytime you see one of those, it feels extra special, you know?"

Mia understood. The rarer the bird, the more exciting the spotting.

When they got back into the car a couple of hours later, Lacy spent some time jotting down things in her purple notebook, telling Mia, "If I don't do it now, I might forget some of the details later."

When Lacy finished writing, she closed the cover with a content smile on her face. "Ah, that was great, wasn't it?"

Mia nodded. "Seeing that bird dive into the water to catch a fish was pretty cool."

"Yep. You just never know what you're going to see. Each time we go, it's different from the last."

"It's like a treasure hunt in a way," Mia said. "Except, instead of precious jewels or pretty shells in the sand, you're looking for different kinds of birds."

Lacy's face lit up. "Exactly! Oh, I'm going to write that

down." She opened her notebook, and as she wrote, she said, "I'm giving you the credit for saying it, of course." When she finished, she said, "I hope you can go next Sunday."

"I already checked with my mom, in case you asked me to go, and she said it's fine."

Lacy clapped her hands together and said, "Yay! I want to get some scrapbook supplies this week so I can start working on making my book." She sighed. "Guess I'll send my assistant out to get some stuff."

Mia started to tell her that it would be more fun for her to go and pick out the stickers and pens and other things herself. Like, what if the assistant didn't think things through and got stickers of dogs when the book was going to be about birds? But before Mia said anything, she remembered that for Lacy, things were different. It was harder for her to do the normal things other girls could do, like go to the craft store and pick out her own stickers.

"Hey," Lacy said, pulling Mia out of her thoughts, "I was wondering, do you have any plans for next Saturday?"

"I have to go and watch my team play soccer in the morning. But after that, I don't have anything going on. Why?"

"I thought I'd check and see," she said as she nervously twisted her ring back and forth on her finger, "if you might want to come and sleep over at my house? Then we could just leave for the lagoon straight from there Sunday morning."

"Oh," Mia said, trying not to sound surprised even though she was sort of freaking out about the idea. "Um . . ."

Stay at Lacy Bell's *house*?

If any of her friends found out, what would they think? And if she said yes, didn't that turn all of this bird watching and photography stuff into something other than a job?

"Never mind," Lacy said, when Mia didn't give an answer right away. "I can tell you don't really want to. It's okay. I shouldn't have asked."

The last thing Mia wanted to do was hurt the girl's feelings. After all, if it weren't for her, Mia wouldn't be here, making money for summer camp doing work that didn't feel like work at all.

"Oh, no, sorry, I do want to," Mia replied quickly. "I was just thinking about whether or not my mom would let me. She's kind of overprotective."

It was like Mia had turned on a light switch by giving Lacy the answer she wanted. Lacy's face was bright and happy again. "My grandma can talk to her. She talked her into letting you come birding with us, right? She's good at that kind of thing." Lacy squeezed Mia's arm. "We're going to have *so* much fun. You'll see."

When they arrived at the café, they all went inside so Gail could speak to Mia's mom about Lacy's idea. While they talked, Lacy gave Mia another hundred-dollar bill.

"Thanks," Mia said. "I'll have more photos for you next weekend."

"I can't wait to see them," Lacy said. "And I get to see you too! For a whole twenty-four hours."

It gave Mia a funny feeling. Like the world had just tilted a little bit and things weren't as they should be. And yet it seemed like, for the moment anyway, there wasn't anything to do but try to get used to it.

When Gail came back and told Mia and Lacy the sleepover was a go, Lacy grabbed Mia and hugged her tight. All Mia could do was close her eyes, hang on, and hope for the best. Whatever that might be.

Chapter 13

white-headed woodpecker
dressed for a party

Mia told herself it was a new week.

A new chance to get things back on track with her friends.

She'd decided she would talk to Salina again and show her she'd been working on her attitude, and everything would go back to normal.

Except when she got to school, the halls were abuzz about something. "What's going on?" Mia asked Josie, who she spotted first when she got to school.

"Tyler Hanks is having a super-cool party this coming weekend," she said. "At the beach. Salina is helping him pass out invitations. She's at your locker; she probably has one for you."

Mia found Salina just where Josie said she'd be. But Mia played it cool and didn't mention the invitation right away.

She figured Salina had probably been looking forward to sharing the exciting news with Mia, and she didn't want to ruin that for her.

"Hey," Mia said. "Everyone seems to be in a really good mood today. What's up with that?"

"Really?" Salina said, looking around. "I hadn't noticed." She avoided meeting Mia's eyes as if they might shoot poisonous darts at her any second. "Look, I gotta go. I need to finish some homework before the bell rings."

"But —"

"Sorry, Mia, but I really do have to go," Salina said before she hurried off down the hall, a fat binder in her hand, no doubt containing the invitations to the super-cool party.

Mia stood there in disbelief. What did Salina's weird behavior mean? Mia felt sick as more and more questions popped into her head.

Had Tyler not invited Mia to the party? And if not, how come? Was it because Salina had told him not to?

She couldn't stand it. Mia decided she had to know what was going on. She went and found Salina's first-period class, language arts, and peered in. Salina's back was to Mia, but she could see her handing an envelope to Jake Evans, who was grinning from ear to ear as he took it from her.

Mia hobbled into the room. All eyes turned to look at her. Salina turned around just as she approached.

"Mia," Salina said. "What are you doing?"

"I think I should be asking you that," Mia said. "Don't I get an invitation?"

"I, uh, well . . ."

Mia blinked back the tears and told herself to stay strong. The last thing she wanted to do was to start crying in this classroom where she didn't even belong.

"Why?" Mia muttered. "Why do you keep leaving me out of things?"

Salina gently grabbed Mia's arm and pulled her out of the room and into the hall. "It's not like that," Salina told Mia. "You have to understand, we're only thinking of you."

"I've known Tyler since I was in kindergarten," Mia said. "Just like you. He would never invite you and not me. What did you say to him?"

"I didn't —"

"What did you say, Salina?" Mia asked, louder this time. She was trying to stay calm, but it wasn't easy.

"There's going to be beach volleyball," Salina said. "And three-legged races. You couldn't do any of that. Would you want us looking over at you all the time, feeling bad? It's a party. It's supposed to be *fun*."

"So you're saying as long as my foot is in this cast, I'm not fun?" Mia quipped back. "How do you even know? We haven't hung out once since I broke my foot. Not a single time. Do you realize that? You act like I've grown three heads — three ugly heads, with bloodshot eyes rolling around in the sockets. It's just a cast. I'm still the same person. You know that, right?"

Salina stood there, her mouth slightly open, like she couldn't quite find the words she was looking for.

"Did you have fun yesterday?" Mia asked. "Surfing?"

"Yeah," Salina said. "We had a blast."

Mia sighed, her shoulders sagging. "So you're afraid I'll ruin things." Mia shook her head. "Thanks. Thanks a lot. I'm so glad our friendship means so much to you."

Mia started to walk away.

"Okay, okay, I'm sorry," Salina called out to her. "I'll get you your invitation, all right?"

Mia shook her head and kept walking. "I don't want it. I'm not going." Then she whispered, "I'm sure that makes you as happy as a lark."

Chapter 14

Red-breasted Nuthatch
a feisty little bird

$\mathcal{M}$ia didn't know where to turn. What to do. She felt so alone.

At lunch, she went straight to the library because she couldn't stand the thought of seeing everyone talking about the party, excited and happy.

She sat at a table in the very back of the room, curled her arms on the table, and rested her head there.

A few minutes later, she felt a tap on her arm. She thought it was probably Mrs. Lennon, wanting to know what was wrong. But when she looked up, it was Josie. Her pretty green eyes looked concerned.

"Hi," Josie said as she sat down across the table.

"Hi."

"Salina told me what happened. Please come and have lunch with us. Please? She feels really bad."

Mia sat back in her chair and crossed her arms. "I can't believe she did that. He actually had an invitation for me, and she told him he shouldn't invite me."

"I know," Josie said. "It was wrong, and she knows it too. She wants to give you your invitation and try to make it up to you."

"I don't want the invitation," Mia said. "I'm not gonna come to the party now anyway, after all that. Besides, I have plans."

Josie gave her a funny look. "You do? Then why'd you get so upset?"

Mia sighed. "Because it hurts to be left out all the time. I feel like you guys would love it if I just . . . disappeared. Which is why I came here instead of the cafeteria today."

"Salina is not going to be happy when she hears that you can't even come to the party after you threw that fit."

"A fit? Is that what she's calling it?" Mia put her face in her hands. "If you're trying to make this better, it's not working."

"I'm sorry," Josie said. She reached over and pulled one of Mia's hands off her face. She squeezed it. "Come with me. Please? If you guys don't make up now, it's just going to get worse and worse every day. Like the laundry basket, when you look at it and it's full and you know you should go and put the clothes in the washer, but you don't. And every time you put more on the pile, you think about what you should do, but you don't, until one day, you have this huge mountain of dirty clothes in your room and nothing to wear."

Mia couldn't help but smile. "You're comparing our friendship to a pile of dirty laundry?"

"No," Josie said, smiling back. "I'm comparing this *fight* to a pile of dirty laundry."

"I've never had a mountain of dirty clothes in my room," Mia said. "Just so you know."

"It'll happen," Josie said. "Someday. I'd bet on it." She raised her eyebrows. "So. You ready to leave this joint and go have some lunch?"

"I don't know," Mia said. "How come Salina didn't come and find me instead of you? I mean, are you sure she even *wants* to talk to me?"

Josie tightened her ponytail as she stood up. "You know what? You are *so* stubborn. Do what you want. I tried. And I'm hungry, so I'm going to go eat my lunch now. Sit in here and be miserable, if that's what you want."

"It just feels horrible to feel left out all the time," Mia tried to explain. "I wish you guys could understand."

"Then be the kind of person we want to include," Josie said.

And with that, she left.

It was another long week. Salina didn't attempt to smooth over Mia's hurt feelings, and Mia avoided her the way birds avoid flying in a hailstorm.

She stayed as far away as she could.

Friday night, Mia and her mother drove to National City, where her dad had been born and raised. Once a month, the two of them went to a big family gathering with Mia's grandparents, aunts, uncles, and cousins. There was always lots of food, games, and conversation. Mia usually looked forward to the get-together, but this time, it was kind of hard to be excited.

As her mother drove, she made small talk, about the weather and the traffic. She reminded her daughter to wish her cousin Raul a happy birthday, since it was coming up in a few days.

"Okay" was all Mia said as she watched the cars inch along on the freeway.

"I don't like seeing you like this," her mother said.

"Like what?" Mia asked.

"*Triste*," her mother replied. "What's happened?"

Sad. So that's how she'd come across at home. Mia hadn't said much to her mother about the situation with her friends. To her mother, the solution would be easy: do whatever you need to do to make up. According to her mother, family and friends were the most important things in the world and you must always do your part to keep them happy.

But Mia didn't feel like backing down. The way Salina had been acting was wrong, and Mia wanted her to really understand that.

"I'm sorry, but I don't want to talk about it," Mia said. "Not now. Maybe some other time."

Her mother patted her daughter's knee. "All right. I bet spending time with your big, happy family will cheer you up."

They certainly couldn't make Mia feel any worse, she thought to herself.

Chapter 15

Flamingo
impossible to hide

After the soccer game on Saturday, Mia went to work with her mother at the café to wait for Lacy to come and pick her up for the sleepover. She brought along a letter from Libby that had arrived in the mail and read it while she ate a sandwich.

Dear Mia,

I was sorry to hear about your broken foot. And just when you should be out there on the field, playing soccer. What bad timing!

I wish there was something I could say or do to cheer you up. You know what they love to say here in the UK, don't you?

Chin up, old chap.

Did that make you smile? I hope so. I can tell you that the picture you sent along of the four of us made me smile like a fool. I miss you all so much, and all of the fun we had together at Camp Brookridge.

I have a couple of new things to tell you since the last time I wrote to you. Remember how I told you, at camp, that my aunt and uncle own a sweet shop? I think when I told you about it, you said a shop filled with candy jars sounded much more fun than a shop filled with coffee, like your mum owns. Well, a new sweet shop will be opening up soon, giving us some competition. My aunt and uncle are furious about it, which means living with them hasn't been very fun lately.

Things with my best friend, Rebecca, haven't improved much. Perhaps it would be easier if we were going to the same school. Speaking of which, things are going all right, I guess, mostly because I've met a boy who's become a new friend. I swear, Mia, that's all — a friend! I met him at the park one day, where he was walking his dog and I was walking Dexter. The funny thing was, Dexter actually liked his dog. I couldn't believe it, because usually Dexter is so mean to other dogs. That's why we started talking, because I told him his dog must be something extra special for Dexter to like him or her. (Now I know it's a girl dog — a blond cocker spaniel named Goldie).

Please write to me and tell me what's new since you last wrote to me! I hope you're finding new ways to have fun. At least you won't have the cast forever, right? Keep telling yourself that!

Your Cabin 7 BFF,

Libby

Yep, Mia thought, that's exactly what she kept telling herself — *the cast is just temporary.* And hopefully, with some luck, all of her weird friend problems would be temporary too.

She stuck the envelope into a pocket of her duffel bag and told herself to make sure and write Libby back soon. She finished her sandwich and checked the time. Just as she did, the door flew open as Lacy rushed in, heading right toward the table where Mia usually sat.

Her smile seemed about as bright as the sun. "Mia!" she exclaimed. "I'm here! Are you ready to go have an *amazing* time?"

Mia gulped as she stood up. "I hope so." She realized that probably wasn't exactly the answer Lacy was looking for. "I mean, yeah, absolutely."

Mia's mom stepped over to where the two girls stood. "You're leaving now?" she asked them.

"Yes," Lacy said. "I had to bring the limo again. It's parked out front." She looked around and then pointed at Mia's bag. "Is this all you have?"

"Oh, was I supposed to bring a sleeping bag? Sorry, I didn't think about that."

Lacy laughed. "A sleeping bag? No, of course not. We're not going camping. Yuck. Can you imagine, sleeping in a tent? On the *ground*? I just thought maybe you had a suitcase or something, but if this is all you have, then great. Let's go!"

Mia grabbed her duffel bag, then gave her mom a kiss on the cheek. "I'll see you tomorrow," she said.

"Please call if anything comes up. Anything at all. *Te quiero*, Mia."

"*Te quiero mucho, Mamá*," Mia replied. She gave her a little wave and then followed Lacy out the door.

It was a beautiful day — warm and sunny. Lacy wore a pretty orange sundress, with gold sandals, and she carried a pretty gold purse. As Mia watched the driver open the car door for Lacy, she felt panic rising up in her chest.

Why had she agreed to do this? To go to a movie star's house and sleep over? She was nothing like Lacy. First of all, Lacy probably never wore the same outfit twice. Second of all, her shoes matched her purse. She *always* carried a purse. If Mia couldn't stick it in the pocket of her shorts or jeans, it stayed home. Third, a limo?! Again?

This is never going to work, Mia thought. *Lacy is way too classy for me. I don't belong with her.*

Lacy peered out of the car at Mia. "What are you doing? Come on, climb in! We managed to lose the paparazzi earlier, but they might show up at any moment. So let's get a move on!"

Maybe Mia could tell Lacy she couldn't go because she suddenly didn't feel well. It was actually kind of true. Her stomach felt queasy as she considered what the next twenty-four hours were going to be like.

"I, um —"

"Did you forget something?" Lacy asked. "You brought along the photos, didn't you? And your camera?"

"Yes," Mia replied. "They're all in my bag. I just, well, I didn't bring any fancy clothes. Like you're wearing."

Lacy waved her hand as if she were swatting away a fly. "Fancy? What do you mean? You don't need anything fancy. We're just going to hang out at my house. Come on, you look fine. Let's rock and roll."

Mia took a deep breath and walked toward the limo. Right before she got in, she heard "Hey, Mia!" from down the sidewalk. She turned and saw Josie, Salina, and Polly walking toward them.

Great, Mia thought. *Perfect timing.*

The last thing Mia wanted to do was explain what she was doing, so Mia gave them a quick wave and then climbed into the limo. The driver quickly shut the door, and a few seconds later, they were on their way.

"Who was that?" Lacy asked. "Some of your friends from school?"

"Yeah," Mia said, grimacing as she thought about the questions she'd have to answer on Monday.

"You could have stayed for a minute and talked to them," Lacy said. "I don't want them to think you're rude or stuck up or something."

"Oh well," Mia said with a sigh. "Too late now."

Chapter 16

Painted Bunting
a spectacular display of colors

*I*t was not a house.

It was a mansion.

An honest-to-goodness mansion, with a chandelier the size of a kiddie pool hanging from the ceiling in the entryway.

"We're here," Lacy called out as she and Mia walked through the set of double doors.

Mia stood there, in awe, feeling like a tiny ant at the bottom of a gigantic hill. She was pretty sure she had never felt so small.

Everything was so pretty. And expensive-looking. The paintings on the walls. The furniture in the living room, or whatever room it was, off to the side from where they stood. The extra-wide staircase that loomed across the room from them.

An older woman with short brown hair and glasses, wearing a simple black dress, came from around a corner somewhere.

"Hi, Alice," Lacy said. "I'd like you to meet Mia. The girl I was telling you about?"

"A pleasure to meet you, Mia," Alice said, smiling. She looked at Lacy. "Shall I have the chef make you anything? Are you hungry?"

Lacy looked at Mia. "I'm fine," Mia said, because that seemed like the most polite response.

"I think we're good for now. Is Mom back yet?" Lacy asked as she slipped her sandals off and picked them up by their straps in one hand. Mia wondered if she should take off her shoe too. Of course she couldn't take off her cast. But they probably didn't want dirt tracked all over their gorgeous house. Mansion. Whatever.

She leaned down and started to untie her sneaker.

"Oh, no," Lacy said. "Don't worry. You're fine. These were just hurting my feet like crazy. Stupid expensive designer shoes." She turned back to Alice. "Sorry, is she back?"

"No," Alice replied. "She called and said she won't be home until quite late tonight. Some friends asked her to meet them for dinner and a show. She told me to tell you to have fun and not to wait up for her. You have an early day tomorrow, since it's birding day."

Lacy sighed. "Okay. Thanks. I guess we'll go upstairs now. Is Mia's room ready?"

"Yes," Alice replied. "It's been prepared exactly as you requested."

"Perfect." She turned to Mia. "Come on. This way."

Mia carried her bag and followed Lacy toward the staircase, thinking how strange it was that Mia would have a room all to herself. This would be a first for her in the sleepover department. She'd slept on the floor, in the bottom bunk of a bunk bed, and even in the same bed with a couple of her cousins when she was younger.

Lacy walked slowly, probably making sure Mia could keep up.

"Your house is beautiful," Mia said to break the awkward silence.

"Thanks," Lacy said. "It's not really my style, but my mom fell in love with the place, and I wanted her to be happy. The pool is pretty sweet, I have to say."

"Sorry I can't swim," Mia said. "Stupid cast."

Lacy was quick to respond. "Oh, no worries. It's fine.

There's lots of other stuff we can do. I think you'll like the theater room."

They reached the top of the stairs, and Mia stared at Lacy, wondering if she'd heard wrong, and said, "Did you say theater room?"

"Yeah. I'll show you later. Follow me."

As Lacy turned to head down the long hallway, Mia told herself to play it cool. She shouldn't freak out over every little thing Lacy told her about or showed her. So Lacy was rich and could afford to live in a mansion with a theater room. Big deal.

Except that was the problem. It kind of *was* a big deal.

Lacy stopped outside a door and said, "This is where you'll sleep. My room is right next door. Go ahead and put your bag away and then come find me, okay? I have to use the little girl's room, but I'll see you in a second."

"Um, since I'll need to go too, eventually, where is the little girl's room?" Mia asked.

"Oh, you have a bathroom all to yourself. There's a door at the far end of your room. You'll see."

Lacy scurried off, leaving Mia alone. She opened the door slowly, almost like she was scared about what she'd find on the other side.

"Wow," she whispered, taking it all in.

There was a king-size bed with more pillows than she'd ever seen on one bed and a beautiful white-and-peach quilt that matched the soft peach walls.

There were vases of brightly colored fresh flowers on every available surface.

There was a chandelier constructed of colorful beads that hung in the middle of the room.

And there was a window seat beneath one of the picture windows made out of a pretty satin fabric.

As Mia put her bag on the bench that sat at the foot of the bed, she noticed a plush white robe. When she picked it up, she saw the yellow *M* sewn on the front.

A personalized robe? For Mia to wear *one* night?

Mia dropped the thing as if it were filled with spiders.

What was Lacy trying to do, make Mia feel like the poorest girl in the state of California? That robe probably cost more than Mia's entire wardrobe.

This was crazy. What was she *doing* here? She belonged here about as much as a giraffe belonged in the ocean.

She found the door at the far end of the room, which she guessed led to the bathroom, stepped inside, and shut the door behind her. Of course the bathroom was gorgeous too, with its pretty silver fixtures and white mar-bled counters. It was huge too. She'd never seen such a large bathtub.

Mia sank onto the floor next to the door and sat there, wishing with all of her heart she hadn't agreed to this sleepover. But it didn't seem like there was any way out, unless she pretended to get sick, and then she wouldn't be able to go birding with them. If she didn't go birding with them, she wouldn't get paid, and she couldn't let that happen.

She made herself stand up and go to one of the sinks, where she splashed water on her face. After she dried off with one of the towels that probably cost hundreds of dollars, she stared at herself in the mirror.

"You can do this," she told herself. "Don't let it get to you. Don't let *her* get to you."

Just then, there was a knock on the door. "Mia, are you in there? Is everything okay?"

Mia went to the door and opened it. "Everything's fine."

Lacy smiled. "Oh, good. When you didn't come find me right away, I started to worry." She turned toward the bedroom. "Do you like it? Aren't the fresh flowers pretty?"

Mia decided she couldn't fake her way out of this. After all, she wasn't an actress like Lacy. If she was really going to stay here for the night, she decided she had to let Lacy know, in the nicest way possible, that this fancy house was kind of freaking her out. "Yes," Mia said. "But I feel a little . . . overwhelmed, to be honest."

Lacy turned back around and stared at Mia. "Oh no. I don't want that. I want you to be happy." She walked over and rubbed Mia's arm. "Please don't let the stuff bother you. It's just stuff, you know?"

"But your stuff is so much nicer than my stuff," Mia said. "The cottage where I live is probably only a little bit bigger than this single room."

Lacy walked over to the bed and sat down with a big sigh. "But see, I love the sound of a beach cottage. It sounds so cute. Like something out of a novel. I don't want you to feel funny about the fancy stuff. So I have a lot of money. So what? My grandpa, who passed away last year, used to say everyone has to put on pants the same way — one leg at a time. Sometimes I wish people would focus not so much on ways we're different, but instead, on the ways that we're the same, you know?"

"Yeah, I guess you're right," Mia said.

"Come on. Wait until you see the surprise I have planned for you." Lacy grinned. "I think you're going to love it!"

For some reason, Mia wasn't so sure about that.

Chapter 17

yellow warbler
easy to spot because of its color

The surprise was a manicure in a room at the far end of the house that looked just like a salon.

No, it didn't look like a salon. It *was* a salon.

"It probably seems weird," Lacy said as she tucked her blond hair behind her ears, "but I spend a lot of time getting my hair, makeup, and nails done. All celebrities do, you know?"

"No, I get it," Mia said, because it did make sense, even if it seemed a little bit over-the-top.

There were two young women sitting at the nail stations. Lacy waved her hand toward them. "I thought we'd get our nails done. Unless you'd like to have your hair done instead? Rhonda does a great job on my hair, I'm sure she would love to do something with yours."

Mia instinctively reached up and touched her hair. "You don't like my hair?"

"No, no, that's not what I meant," Lacy said. "I just . . . I want you to be happy. So what will it be? Nails or hair?"

Nails or hair? Never, in the history of her life, had Mia been asked such a simple question and been unable to figure out the right answer. She looked down at her nails, which seemed so boring and simple, like the rest of her, and realized she'd never had her fingernails painted. Ever. It just wasn't her thing.

Being girly, in general, wasn't really her thing.

But she liked her hair, long and wavy and easy to put into a ponytail. What if Rhonda decided to do something trendy and gave her some freaky cut?

"Nails, I guess," Mia said.

"Great!" Lacy said, plopping down into one of the chairs and putting both her hands up on to the table. "We can sit here and get to know each other better."

Mia sat down in the other chair and put her hands out the way Lacy had.

"That's Tawni, by the way," Lacy said.

"Hi," Mia said to Tawni. "Thanks for doing this."

"My pleasure," she said as she placed both of Mia's hands

into a bowl of warm, soapy water. "Do you want to choose a color or would you like clear polish?"

"Clear will be fine," Mia said.

"Are you sure?" Lacy asked. "They just got the prettiest shade of yellow in last week. That's what I want."

Mia wrinkled her face. "Yellow?"

"I know, it sounds kind of strange for a nail color, but just wait. I saw pictures in a magazine of models with pastel-yellow fingernails, and it looked amazing."

"So, are you sticking with clear?" Tawni asked. Mia nodded. Tawni smiled as she picked up Mia's left hand and went to work massaging some kind of oil onto each of Mia's fingernails.

"We actually have a lot in common, you know," Lacy said as she leaned back in her chair as if she might actually be trying to relax for once. Mia felt herself relaxing into her own chair too.

"We do?" Mia asked. "Like what?"

"Like, we're both only children. At least, I assume you're an only since you haven't mentioned any siblings."

Mia nodded. "I am."

"And we both have single mothers." Lacy paused. "Right?"

There was no getting out of it this time. "Right," Mia said matter-of-factly.

A look of satisfaction washed across Lacy's face. "And we both love the beach. I don't surf like you do, but the beach is one of my favorite places. It is for you too, right?"

Mia nodded. "For sure."

Just then, a nicely dressed young woman scurried into the room, holding a phone. "Lacy, there's a call you need to take."

Lacy went from relaxed to fired-up-and-ready in the blink of an eye. She leaned forward, her, brows furrowed together. "Danielle, didn't I tell you to hold all of my calls? I don't want to talk to anyone while Mia's here."

"I know," she said. "And I'm sorry. But this is important. It's about your lines for next week."

Rhonda quickly dried off Lacy's hands, and then Lacy stood up. "I am so sorry," she told Mia. "I'll be right back."

"No problem."

After she left, Mia watched Tawni as she took great care to clip each cuticle with a special little tool.

"I'm glad you're here," Tawni said, glancing up to meet Mia's eyes briefly before returning to her work. "She talks about you all the time. You're the first friend she's had in a long time."

"What do you mean?" Mia asked.

Rhonda stood up and stretched, twisting her body right and then left. "She means, it's hard for a celebrity to make friends. People don't know how to act around her. After all, her life is different, yes? She's lonely quite a bit. Of course, she works a lot, so she doesn't have time to think about it much. But when she does, it's sad to see her realizing what she's missing."

Tawni picked up a finger file and began filing Mia's nails. "I think it's wonderful that you've been able to get past her celebrity status. It's easy to get hung up on the superficial stuff and forget that deep down inside, Lacy is a just a regular thirteen-year-old girl with hopes and dreams and insecurities like everyone else."

Mia sat there, quietly, taking it all in and trying to figure out what it all meant.

You're the first friend she's had in a long time.

How come Mia hadn't realized it before now? The flowers, the bathrobe, the manicure — Lacy wasn't showing off. She wasn't trying to make Mia feel bad about herself and her situation. No, it was something much different. Lacy was simply trying to do nice things for Mia because she viewed her as a friend.

It was all in the name of friendship.

While Mia felt somewhat relieved by this discovery, she also felt something else. Uncertainty. For up until now, Mia had viewed Lacy more like an employer than a friend. Could Mia be what Lacy really needed? Could she be Lacy's friend?

She looked down at the pretty charm bracelet on her wrist as she thought of her three friends from camp: Caitlin, Libby, and Hannah. They were each so different and yet, they had become really good friends.

The best of friends, in fact.

If one of them were here, giving Mia advice about the situation, she was pretty sure they would tell her she should give it a chance.

After all, what did she really have to lose?

Chapter 18

Emu
might give you nightmares

$\mathcal{L}$acy had been right. The pastel-yellow nails looked super cute.

As for Mia's nails, they'd never looked so good. She had to admit, having a manicure was pretty awesome. Before Tawni had painted Mia's nails, she gave Mia's hands a nice massage with lotion. It felt *so* good.

After their nails were done, Lacy gave Mia a tour of the rest of the house. When they went into the kitchen, they met the chef, Suki, who wore a cheerful pink-and-green apron and smiled at Mia like she was the queen of England, and then proceeded to give Mia a big hug and a kiss on the cheek, as if they'd known each other forever.

"Is there anything special you'd like to have for dinner?" she asked the girls.

Lacy looked at Mia. "You choose. You're the guest."

"Oh, wow, I don't know. Anything's fine. Really."

"She makes the most delicious chicken fettuccini you've ever had," Lacy said. "How's that sound?"

Mia nodded. "Sure. That's great."

"What about dessert?" Suki asked. She reached over and put her arm around Lacy's shoulders. "I know you usually don't have dessert, but come on, live a little."

The words tumbled out of Mia's mouth before she had a chance to think about it. "Do you know how to make a fruit pizza?"

Suki grinned. "Of course. Cookie crust, a cream-cheese filling, and covered in fresh fruit, right?"

"Yes!" Mia said. "I had it at summer camp for the first time, and I've been dying to have it again."

"Oh, how fun," Lacy said as she clapped her hands together. "We can have a tiny taste of summer camp right here in my house."

"Fruit pizza it is, then," Suki said. "I'll have dinner ready for you at six. Do you want anything to snack on in the meantime? Some veggies and dip, maybe?"

"Yes, please," Lacy said. "We'll take it up to my room."

Suki pulled out a big plastic tub filled with vegetables and went to work making a veggie plate.

"I figure now that you've had the official tour, we can

hang out in my room until dinner," Lacy explained. "I want to show you what I've done so far with my scrapbook. After dinner, I thought we might watch a movie."

"Okay," Mia said.

The girls thanked Suki for the snack and then headed back to Lacy's room. Mia had only peeked into her room briefly as they made their way around the house, but now, they went in and settled in on the black leather sofa that sat in front of the flat-screen television on the wall.

Mia could hardly get over it — a bedroom big enough to have all the normal bedroom stuff *plus* a couch, a coffee table, and a flat-screen TV. Lacy placed the plate of veggies and dip in between them and they started munching.

"If you want a peanut butter and jelly sandwich," Mia asked, "can you go into the kitchen and make one, or does Suki make everything for you?"

Lacy licked her lips. "Yum. I haven't had a peanut butter and jelly sandwich in forever."

Mia scrunched up her face. "Seriously? So I guess that means you don't really do much in the kitchen, then."

"Probably because I don't need to. If I want something to eat, Suki gets it for me. It's pretty much her job, you know?"

"What about late-night snacks?" Mia asked. "Even chefs have to sleep."

Lacy shrugged. "I've never had a late-night snack. I'm usually in bed by ten. Eleven at the latest, if I don't have to work the next day. What do you even eat for a late-night snack? I have no idea."

Mia finished her celery stick and reached for a carrot. "Well, I usually have cookies and warm milk, because warm milk makes a person sleepy. It's what I do if I wake up from a nightmare and can't go back to sleep."

Lacy shook her head and tried to smile. "If I have a nightmare, I usually turn on the TV until I can go back to sleep. Am I the weirdest person you've ever met or what?"

"No," Mia said. "Definitely not the weirdest. Cesar Lagunas, a kid at my school, he's the weirdest. He puts ketchup on everything. I've even seen him put it on ice cream."

"Ew," Lacy said, scrunching up her nose. "Are you serious?"

"Totally. It's disgusting. He should be on that TV show about strange addictions. Have you seen that?"

"Ohmygosh, yes!" Lacy shrieked. "If I come across that show, I can't turn away, no matter how gross it is. Did you see the one where the guy couldn't stop licking his cat?"

"Ack, no!" Mia said, laughing. "Now see, that is weird. You're not weird. Not even close to weird. You're just famous, that's all. And, you know . . . rich."

"Some days I wish I wasn't," Lacy said softly. "You can't even begin to imagine how lonely it is sometimes. Even though I have a person for just about everything, they're all adults, and they do what they do for me basically because they have to. You know, because it's their job."

Mia didn't know what to say. "I'm sorry it's like that for you."

Lacy took the veggie tray and placed it on the coffee table, since both of them had stopped eating. "You don't know how lucky you are, Mia. You have your camp friends and your school friends. So many friends. I really don't have anyone. Not like that."

"Except I'm not getting along with some of my friends at school right now." Mia groaned slightly as she leaned back into the sofa. "It's no fun, let me tell you."

"I still think you're lucky," Lacy said. Then she shook her head, like she didn't want to think about it anymore. "Okay, let me get my scrapbook and show you what I've done so far. I think you're going to love it."

As she got up and went over to a desk, Mia thought about what Lacy had said.

Lucky.

Mia glanced at the charm bracelet she wore. Lucky could mean a lot of different things. The more she thought about it, the more she realized Lacy was right. Mia *was* lucky. Or maybe fortunate was a better word. Because Mia knew she wouldn't trade her friendships for all of the limos and salons and flat-screen TVs in the world. And suddenly, she couldn't wait to make up with Salina when she got back home.

Chapter 19

Elf Owl
a fan of the night

The chicken fettuccini was to die for.

And the fruit pizza was out of this world. Lacy loved it too. As the two girls talked and laughed and ate, Mia realized she hadn't had this much fun in a long, long time.

After dinner, they watched two movies back-to-back, while eating Red Vines (a mutual favorite). When the movies were over, Lacy got up and turned on the lights. Mia looked around the theater room, with a screen in the front and two rows of chairs, just like a real movie theater, and said, "That was great. This is how everyone should watch movies at home."

"I'm glad you liked it," Lacy said, stifling a yawn. She looked at the clock on the wall. "We should probably get to bed. You know, since we have to get up with the birds."

Mia smiled. "You sound like your grandma."

They walked to their rooms and when they reached the door to Mia's room, Lacy said, "I hope you sleep all right. If you have a nightmare, come and wake me. We'll go and have cookies and milk together."

"We could go have some now," Mia said. "Then you can be in the late-night snack club."

Lacy's eyes sparkled. "Oooh, yes, let's do it!"

As they made their way to the kitchen, Lacy looped her arm through Mia's and said, "I'm so glad we met that first day at the café. Because I really like you, Mia Cruz."

Mia replied, "Well, I like you too, Lacy Bell. Especially because you don't lick cats."

The two girls laughed and laughed.

The next morning, Suki made the girls omelets. As she placed their plates in front of them at the dining room table, she said, "I found a few crumbs on the counter that weren't there when I left last night. I wonder, do we have mice, or did the two of you have a late-night snack?"

"It was us," Lacy said with a smile. "You aren't mad, are you? I'd never had a late-night snack before. We had cookies and warm milk. Mia heated up the milk on the stove, in a pan, and made it slightly warm, not too hot. It was good."

Suki crossed her arms and tried to look angry. "Well, how dare you girls. Don't you know if you're going to have a late-night snack, you're supposed to invite me along? That's just about my most favorite meal of the day." She smiled as she reached over and patted Lacy's arm. "I'm so glad Mia's teaching you how to live a little."

There it was again. That phrase, "live a little." As if Lacy's celebrity life wasn't living at all. It seemed so strange to Mia.

After Suki returned to the kitchen, Mia asked, "Will I get to meet your mom? I mean, does she get up to see you before you go birding?"

Lacy took a sip of orange juice. "No. I never see her in the mornings. She's not a morning person. At all."

"Oh," Mia said, thinking of her own mom and how she arranged her schedule so she could be with Mia every morning before school and on Saturdays for her soccer games. She'd hate to have to get up all by herself every day and leave the house without seeing her mom. Once again, Mia found herself feeling bad for Lacy.

Before they could say anything more about it, Gail

marched into the dining room, carrying the bag she brought along every week that held their binoculars and notebooks.

"Good morning, my fine feathered friends," she said as she took a seat next to Lacy. "You both look well. Have fun yesterday, did you?"

"Yes," the girls answered at the exact same time.

"Wonderful," Gail said. "Splendid. Happy to hear it. I think I shall go pester Suki for some coffee and a bit of food while you girls finish up. Then we can just head to the lagoon straight away. I'll be back in a jiffy."

As she left, Mia took another bite of her delicious omelet. "I could get used to eating Suki's food, that's for sure."

"Anytime you want to come over and eat something, just let me know," Lacy said. "She won't mind at all. And I'd love it, of course."

"Okay, I'll remember that," Mia said. "When I'm craving fruit pizza, I'll just give you a call."

"Please do," Lacy said. "I'm totally serious. In the car, let's make sure to exchange phone numbers, okay?"

"Lacy, it's so rude though," Mia said, laughing. "Calling up someone to come and eat their food?"

"No, it's not rude at all. Not when it's you. It's friendly, and it means you're comfortable with me, which is awesome."

"Awesome," Mia repeated. "Now you're even talking like me."

"I think you should just move in here," Lacy said, finishing her last bite of breakfast. "Honestly, it feels like you belong here with me."

Mia didn't know what to say to that, so she didn't say anything. She knew Lacy was joking, but still, it was sad how lonely the poor girl seemed to be. Thankfully, Gail came strolling in carrying a mug of coffee and a bagel.

"All right, my little chickadees, are we ready to go?" Gail asked before she took a sip of her coffee.

"We're ready," Lacy said. "Mia's stuff is by the front door, Grandma, can you ask the driver to put it in the car?"

"Already taken care of," Gail said. "So let's skedaddle, shall we?"

As they walked to the car, Mia thought about how she'd known Gail and Lacy for only a couple of weeks, and yet, in some ways, it seemed like she'd known them forever.

Like old friends.

It was the best expedition yet. They saw many, many birds, and Mia took literally hundreds of pictures.

"There's something special about today," Gail said as they rose from the bench where they'd been sitting. "I wonder what it is."

Lacy looked at Mia and said, "I couldn't agree more."

And just then, when it didn't seem like the day could get any better, Gail turned to them with her finger on her lips and whispered, "Shhh. Girls, listen."

Everyone stood completely still, not saying a word. The sound they heard was like an old beater of a car, sputtering down the road.

Lacy's eyes got really big as she mouthed the words, *clapper rail.*

Mia felt goose bumps popping up all over her arms. Gail's life bird was close. Really close! But where? Where was it?

Gail put the binoculars to her eyes and scanned the area ever so slowly. Lacy was looking too. It seemed like an eternity before she finally pointed her finger at a bird that had just come out from the grassy marsh and was now strutting along the shore, next to the water. Mia zoomed in with her camera and took picture after picture. It was a good-size bird, with funny looking feet and a skinny orange beak. Mia watched as it jumped into the water and gave itself a bath. The bird put its head into the water, then wiggled its whole body as it rubbed its wing with its beak. The bird did it over and over again. Lacy let out a little giggle at the sight.

When the bird finished bathing, it got back on shore and walked a little more before it ducked back into the marsh and disappeared.

Gail lowered her binoculars and hit her thigh with her hand. "Now, wasn't that just something to crow about?"

Lacy ran to her grandmother and gave her a big hug. "We did it, Grandma. We really did it! We finally saw the bird you've been dreaming about."

Gail looked like she was about ready to cry. Mia was so honored to have been part of that special moment.

"What'd you think, Mia?" Gail asked her. "Does the light-footed clapper rail have another fan now?"

"I thought it was amazing," Mia said. "Knowing how long you've been trying to find that bird, it was the best feeling knowing you finally got your wish."

"I can hardly believe it," Gail said.

"I totally get it," Lacy said, holding Gail's hand. "It's how I felt last night, sitting across the table from Mia, having a late-night snack with my new friend. Like you just want to

stop time because it doesn't seem like it w_
ter than that."

*   *   *

On the ride to the café, Gail and Lacy scribbled notes in their notebooks as Mia sat and thought about how much things had changed since the first time she met Lacy and her grandma.

Birding wasn't weird at all. It was fun. Exciting. Never in a million years would Mia have believed it if someone told her that, but she'd seen it for herself.

And then there was Lacy. Just like Mia had made assumptions about what bird watching would be like, she'd made assumptions about what Lacy would be like. And most of it hadn't been true. Deep down, Lacy was a regular girl, just like Mia, who wanted what everyone ultimately wants — for people to understand her and to care about her.

When they pulled up to the café, Lacy got out her purse like she'd done every other time. Mia felt her heartbeat quicken as she thought about taking Lacy's money. It didn't seem right anymore, after everything Lacy had done for her over the weekend.

"Please," Lacy said, extending her hand with the money. "Take it. I can tell you're thinking you shouldn't this time, want you to have it. You took a ton of photos today and you earned it. Really."

Mia hesitated another second before she reached out and took the hundred-dollar bill. "Thank you," she said. "For everything."

"No," Lacy said. "Thank *you* for everything. This was the best weekend I've had in a really long time."

"Will we see you next Sunday morning?" Gail asked.

"I hope so," Mia said. "I'll have lots of pictures of your friend, the light-footed clapper rail."

Gail rubbed her hands together. "Oh dear me, I can hardly wait."

The driver opened the door, and as Mia climbed out of the limo, she was shocked when she came face-to-face with about twenty kids from her school. Not only that, but Salina and Josie were front and center. All of them bombarded her with questions.

"Does she take a limo wherever she goes?"

"Can you get us her autograph to sell online?"

"Are you too good for us now, Mia?"

"What's it like to be friends with a *rich* girl?"

Mia stood there, squeezing her fists, trying to stay calm. But it was *so* hard. After basically ignoring her last week, now they wanted to talk to her, just so they could make fun of her?

Mia couldn't take it. She yelled, "Stop it! She's not my friend, okay? Like I said before, I work for her. I take photos." She held up her camera and the hundred-dollar bill. "See?"

It was quiet for just a second before the noise started up again. And in that second, Mia realized the driver hadn't shut the car door yet, because he'd been getting her bag.

Lacy had heard everything Mia had said.

Chapter 20

Emperor Penguin
picture-perfect

Mia watched the limo drive away, feeling sick. Like the way she felt after crashing in a big wave, swallowing a bunch of seawater, and having to return to the shore feeling small and defeated.

What had she done?

With the celebrity show now over, most of the kids headed across the street, toward the beach. Salina and Josie stuck around.

Mia looked at them. "What are you even doing here?"

"After we saw you yesterday," Josie said, "we asked your mom where you were going. She said you were sleeping over at Lacy's house. When we asked what time you'd be back, she told us. Mia, why didn't you tell us?"

"Probably because I was afraid of something like

this," Mia said. "Why did you have to tell half the school?"

"We didn't," Josie said. "I mean, not really. I think maybe we each told a few people, and I guess they told a few people . . ."

Mia picked up her bag. "Well, I hope you got what you came for." She looked at Salina. "Was the party fun yesterday?"

Salina crossed her arms. "Yeah. It was. I don't know why you were so mad about that whole thing. You obviously had better things to do anyway."

Furious, Mia squeezed the handle of her bag tightly. She tried to keep her voice low and calm as she said, "It's still nice to be invited."

"Come on, you guys," Josie said. "Make up already. Salina, I thought you were going to apologize."

"Okay. I'm sorry," Salina muttered, her voice so quiet Mia could barely hear her. It was the most pathetic apology in the history of disagreements.

"Great. Thanks," Mia said, not too convincingly. "Look, I gotta go. I'll see you at school on Tuesday, since tomorrow's a holiday."

She walked toward the door of the café. "We want to

125

hear all about it, you know," Josie said. "What Lacy's house is like. What you guys did. If she's as in love with herself as she seems to be. That kind of stuff."

Mia didn't respond. She kept walking until she was inside the quiet, and thankfully empty, café.

Her mother smiled, happy to see her. Mia rushed over, dropped her bag, and fell into her mother's loving arms. It made Mia feel better. At least a little bit, anyway.

Mia tried calling Lacy approximately seventeen times. She texted her three times.

The first time: **Please let me explain. Please? Call me.**

The second time: **I'm so sorry. I want to talk to you about it.**

The third time: **Lacy, I feel horrible. I didn't mean it. Please believe me!**

Maybe Lacy's assistant still had her phone. Or maybe she was busy practicing lines for work. Or maybe she never wanted to speak to Mia again. How could Mia blame her, really?

After dinner, Mia went to her room and pulled out a piece of paper and a pen and began writing.

Dear Libby,

Thanks for your letter! I love how hard you were trying to cheer me up. I miss you SO much.

I have a lot to tell you, but I don't even know where to start. I know, I know, I should start at the beginning.

Do you know who Lacy Bell is? She's a famous teen actress here in America. Well, she came into the café one Sunday morning with her grandma, and when she saw my camp photos, she asked if I'd go with them and take photos while they watched for birds. I know, it sounds crazy. But she promised to pay me, and so I went, and I actually had fun. It's pretty cool, seeing the different birds and identifying them and looking for the ones that are harder to find. I've gone with them three times now and each time it gets better and better. It's really peaceful out there with nothing but nature all around you. I know you'll understand, because I remember how much you loved the nature hikes at camp.

Anyway, I stayed at her house this past weekend, and I got to know her better. She's really nice and we had a lot of fun. I probably haven't had that

MUCH FUN SINCE CAMP BROOKRIDGE. SHE SAID I COULD COME BACK WHENEVER I WANTED.

SO BASICALLY, WE BECAME FRIENDS.

THE SAD THING IS THAT I DIDN'T WANT TO ADMIT IT. KIDS SAY MEAN THINGS ABOUT HER, LIKE THEY DO ABOUT A LOT OF CELEBRITIES, YOU KNOW? AND I DIDN'T WANT THEM SAYING THOSE THINGS ABOUT ME.

BUT NOW I KNOW THAT WE'RE FRIENDS. OR WERE. I'M NOT SURE. BECAUSE I'VE DONE SOMETHING HORRIBLE. I TOLD A BUNCH OF KIDS FROM SCHOOL THAT WE AREN'T FRIENDS, AND SHE HEARD ME SAY IT.

LIBBY, WHAT AM I GOING TO DO? SHE WON'T ANSWER MY CALLS OR TEXTS. MY MOM SAYS MAYBE AFTER SHE HAS TIME TO COOL DOWN, SHE'LL CALL ME BACK. SHE TELLS ME I JUST NEED TO GIVE HER TIME AND SPACE. BE PATIENT. BUT IT'S SO HARD.

I WISH I COULD GO BACK IN TIME AND DO THE WHOLE THING OVER. THERE REALLY SHOULD BE A REWIND BUTTON FOR LIFE.

I NEED THIS LUCKY BRACELET TO WORK NOW MORE THAN EVER. I DON'T WANT TO LOSE MY NEW FRIEND, LIBBY. LIKE CAITLIN SAID IN HER LETTER TO ME A WHILE BACK, SOMETIMES AWESOME SHOWS UP WHEN YOU LEAST EXPECT IT.

I DIDN'T EXPECT LACY BELL TO BE AWESOME, BUT SHE IS, AND SHE CAME ALONG AT JUST THE RIGHT TIME — WHEN I REALLY NEEDED A FRIEND. I HOPE I CAN MAKE THINGS RIGHT.

I KNOW THIS LETTER IS ALL ME, ME, ME, BUT RIGHT NOW, I DON'T REALLY HAVE ANYONE TO TALK TO ABOUT THIS. THANKS FOR LISTENING.

YOUR CABIN 7 BFF,
MIA
PS. WHAT'S YOUR FRIEND'S NAME? THE ONE WHO OWNS GOLDIE? YOU TOLD ME THE DOG'S NAME BUT NOT YOUR FRIEND'S. I DON'T KNOW WHY, BUT I FIND THAT REALLY FUNNY.

After she finished getting the letter ready to mail, Mia went and asked her mom if she could use her printer to print out a few photos. Her mom preferred going to the drugstore, because ink for her little printer wasn't cheap, but she did have some photo paper and said it would be okay this one time as long as she didn't do too many.

Mia hooked her camera up to the computer and browsed the pictures. She stopped when she came to one where Lacy had looked right at the camera and put her hands together in the shape of the heart. The soft blue sky and bright green vegetation was behind her, making it a visually pretty picture, but the main thing Mia noticed was how truly happy Lacy looked. How many moments did she get like that, in her busy and lonely life?

Mia knew the answer to that. Not many.

Mia suddenly wished she had one of her and Lacy together. Why hadn't she asked Gail to take one of the two of them?

She printed out the photo of Lacy making the heart, along with one of her and her grandma as they watched the clapper rail with pure joy on their faces, and finally, the best one of the clapper rail she'd taken, as it stood in the water, taking a bath.

Back in her room, Mia took a frame from her dresser that held three pictures of her with her mom and went to work putting the three pictures she'd printed out into the frame instead. When she finished, she stood back and admired it. She'd get the rest of the photos developed at the drugstore, like always. But in addition to what she normally gave to Lacy, she'd have something extra special to give to her as well.

She could only hope it would be enough to fix the mess she'd made.

Chapter 21

Hummingbird
a tiny treasure

Monday was Columbus Day, so Mia didn't have school. Her mom had to work though, so she took her scrapbook and supplies to the café along with her camera, for a walk on the beach later.

Lacy still hadn't returned Mia's calls, and Mia had decided it was probably best to do as her mom had suggested and back off for now. She didn't want to annoy her any more than she already had. Hopefully by Sunday Lacy wouldn't be as hurt, and Mia could explain and give her the framed photos as an apology gift.

The café was pretty busy. Mia offered to help her mom, but she told her to sit and relax. So Mia worked away on her scrapbook while her mom worked away serving up coffee and muffins.

And then, they had a surprise customer. Salina. Except she didn't appear to be there for drink or food.

"Hi," Salina said, standing at Mia's table. "I thought I'd probably find you here."

"Yep."

"What are you working on?"

"I'm trying to finish up a scrapbook."

Salina picked up a photo of Libby, Hannah, and Caitlin standing in front of the Pink Giraffe, the day they found the charm bracelet. "Is this from camp?" she asked.

"Yes. They all are."

"Looks like fun," she said, setting the photo back down.

"It was," Mia said, kind of wondering when Salina was going to tell her what she was doing here.

Salina looked around at the bustling café and said, "Could we maybe go for a walk? On the beach?"

"Okay. Let me put this stuff away first."

With the table cleaned up and the supplies stored away, the girls headed off toward the beach. Outside, it was a bit cooler than it had been lately, and Mia was glad she'd brought a jacket along. Salina zipped up her yellow hoodie.

"I wanted to tell you, I kind of figured out something this weekend," Salina said.

Mia looked at her. "What?"

"Wait," she said. "Maybe I figured out a couple of things. Anyway, the first thing is that, you were right. I was wrong. I was leaving you out of things. Not on purpose though. Like, I didn't set out to hurt your feelings or anything. It just sort of . . . happened. Things were suddenly so different, with your foot in a cast, and yeah, I didn't think about how hard on you it must have been. And I'm sorry."

"You are?" Mia asked, wanting to hear it again.

"I really am."

It felt like a bunch of bricks were lifted off Mia's shoulders. Finally, they were talking again. Maybe, just maybe, things were on the right track. "What's the other thing?" Mia asked.

They got to the beach and just like before, it was hard for Mia to walk in the soft sand.

Salina watched Mia struggle. "You must be *so* sick of that thing."

"Eight more days," Mia replied. "I can't believe it. For so long, it felt like it was a hundred years away. I guess staying busy with Lacy has helped the time fly."

The girls made their way toward the water. Mia took in

a deep breath of sea air and felt herself finally relaxing after all of the stress from the past twenty-four hours.

"So the other thing," Salina said as they walked, "is that I've missed you. When I heard you had a sleepover with Lacy, I kind of got . . . jealous. Like, I kept wondering, why wasn't it me who was having a sleepover with you?"

"Maybe because you didn't invite me?" Mia asked with a hint of a smile, trying not to sound too smug.

"I know, I know, it's crazy, because you're right," Salina said before she laughed. "And now I feel silly that I felt jealous at all since you two aren't really friends, just like you said yesterday."

Oh no, Mia thought. *Here we go.*

They reached the hard, wet sand and Mia saw a sand dollar sticking out of the sand. She reached down and gave it a soft, careful tug.

Usually Mia found broken ones, so what a surprise when she discovered that this one was almost perfect.

"Wow," Salina said, looking on. "It's hard to find ones that look as good as that."

Mia brushed off the sand as she turned it over in her hands. "What a treasure," she whispered. It made her think of what her mother had said after Caitlin had mailed Mia the bracelet along with homemade cookies.

Good friends are a treasure.

"I think there's something I realized this weekend too," Mia said, turning and facing Salina.

"Yeah? What's that?"

"I realized I like having friends. Different kinds of friends, for doing different kinds of things. And maybe Lacy is different than most girls in a lot of ways, but she's also the same in some ways too. I was embarrassed to say it yesterday, with everyone standing there, but she *is* my friend."

"She is?" Salina asked.

"Yeah. She is. And there's something else. The bird books I checked out, at the library? They weren't for my mom, they were for me. Lacy and I have been going bird-watching together, and it's fun. I know it probably sounds kind of strange, but I really like doing it, and I want to keep doing it. I hope you can be okay with that."

Salina turned to walk down the beach, and Mia did the same. "So Lacy's nice?" Salina asked. "Not stuck up or whatever?"

"She's super nice. And lonely, because it's hard for her to make friends. Salina, she lives in this incredible mansion with all these cool things, and she's actually jealous of *me*. Do you know why?"

Salina shook her head. "No. Why?"

"Because I play soccer and have friends and can go to the mall anytime I want without being mobbed by people."

"Really? Wow. I guess I never thought of it like that."

The two didn't say anything for a while. They just walked along, scanning the sand for more treasures.

Salina reached down and picked up a shiny golden agate with little black specks.

"It's pretty," Mia said.

"Not as cool as yours," Salina replied.

"They're different," Mia said. "That's all. Just think how boring the beach would be if all you found were sand dollars." She paused. "And how boring the world would be if all you found were girls who like to surf."

Salina stopped. "Wait. What? That'd be pretty awesome, wouldn't it?"

"The ocean would be way too crowded," Mia said. "It'd be horrible."

Salina gave Mia a little shove. "Okay, okay, I get your point."

Mia laughed, and Salina joined in.

"I'm so glad we're here," Salina said. "Doing this. Looking

for treasures. Talking. Do you think — I mean, would you want to sleep over this weekend?"

"Sure, if it's on Friday night," Mia said. "I have plans on Sunday, so Saturday wouldn't work. Well, at least I *hope* I have plans on Sunday. I may have messed everything up with Lacy now, after she heard what I said. I think I really hurt her feelings."

"Welcome to the club."

"The club?"

"The club of hurting people's feelings," Salina said. "It's not a fun place to be."

"Well, you're out of the club now," Mia said. "Since everything's better between us. You need to start a new club now. Something more fun."

"Pigs-in-a-bunk bed club?" Salina asked.

It sounded so ridiculous, Mia couldn't help but laugh. "Yes. Perfect. Hopefully I can join you there soon."

"We'll go out for breakfast to celebrate," Salina said. "How's that sound?"

"Awesome," Mia said.

And she really meant it.

Chapter 22

Mallard Duck
an excellent Swimmer

$\mathcal{M}$ia and Lacy Bell were the talk of the school on Tuesday.

Kids wanted to know *everything*.

And Mia didn't want to say a thing about it.

Fortunately, Salina and Josie stuck close to Mia, and together the three girls got the word out that Mia wouldn't be talking about Lacy. At all. They could ask all the questions they wanted, but that didn't mean Mia would be answering them.

Eventually, the whole thing died down and things were back to normal.

When Sunday arrived, Mia woke up extra early, too nervous to sleep. She'd gotten last week's pictures developed and there were some really great shots. She sat on her bed, flipping through them, remembering how much fun they'd had. As she stared at one she'd taken of an osprey in flight, she thought of Lacy, wanting to be free like that but feeling so trapped in her life.

It made Mia's heart ache even more, thinking about how she'd hurt Lacy. She became more determined than ever to make everything right.

After she showered and got ready, she waited for her mom in the family room.

"Excited to see your friend today?" her mother asked her as she gathered her purse and keys from the coffee table.

"I guess you could say that," Mia said as they left the cottage and walked out to the car. "Nervous too, though. She might still be upset about what happened. I just hope I can make things right."

"I'm sure you can," her mother said. "I'm glad this job has worked out so well for you," her mother said.

They got in the car and buckled up. "Well," Mia said. "It's not going to be a job any longer. I'm going to tell Lacy today that she's my friend and that means I can't take her money anymore. I want to keep bird-watching with her, but not to get paid. It's fun, and I don't mind taking photos."

Her mom didn't say anything.

"Hopefully, I can find another way to pay for camp," Mia said. "It'll be okay."

"*Sí*," her mother said. "It's the right thing, what you're doing. I'm proud of you, Mia. It's not always easy to do the right thing."

Mia sighed. "You don't have to tell me that."

She waited and waited for Gail and Lacy to arrive. Just when she thought they wouldn't be coming, she saw the town car pull up in front of the café. Unable to contain her excitement, she got up and hobbled to the front door and opened it, ready to greet Gail and Lacy.

Gail got out of the car and waved. Mia waved back. Gail didn't wait by the car, and the driver didn't get out to open the door like he usually did for Lacy.

That's when it hit Mia — Gail had come alone.

Mia didn't even try to hide her disappointment.

"So sorry, my dear," Gail said after she stepped inside the café. "Lacy isn't feeling well, so she stayed home today. I stopped by to get the photos because we've both been looking forward to seeing them."

Mia swallowed hard, taking in this news. Lacy had made up an excuse so she wouldn't have to come. Mia reached for the bracelet she wore and rubbed the flower charm, hoping it would make her feel better.

"The photos are over here," Mia said softly, "At the table. Let me get them."

As she handed the envelopes to Gail, Mia said, "Did she say anything else? Like, did she have a message for me or anything?"

"I'm afraid not, no," Gail said. Her brown eyes looked kind. And maybe a little concerned.

Mia plopped down in the chair. "I can't believe this." Her eyes filled with tears but she blinked them back. "She's upset with me. And I need to talk to her. Explain things, you know? I even have a special gift I want to give her. I can't believe she didn't come with you."

"I'm sorry it's such a pickle," Gail said as she reached out and rubbed Mia's back.

Mia had an idea, but she wasn't sure Gail would go for it. Or even her mother, for that matter. Still, it seemed like her only chance, so she had to try.

"Could you take me to see her?" Mia asked. "Please? I know it would probably mean no bird watching for you today, and I'm really sorry."

Gail nodded, the lines of her eyes crinkling again as she gave Mia a smile. "We had such a fine time last Sunday, I suppose today was bound to pale in comparison anyway. I would be happy to take you to see Lacy. I hate to see her unhappy, and she has seemed pretty miserable all week. Shall we check with the mother hen to make sure she's agreeable to the idea?"

"Let me go and ask her," Mia said. "If I need your help, I'll let you know."

"Certainly," Gail said.

Mia went in the back and found her mother, who was mixing up a new batch of muffins. "*Mamá*, Gail is here, but Lacy stayed home. I really need to talk to her, so Gail said the driver could take the two of us back to her house. That's all right with you, isn't it?"

Mia's mother put the spatula down and wiped her hands on a towel. "Are you sure this is such a good idea? If she'd wanted to see you today, she would have come with Gail."

"I have to talk to her," Mia said. "I just have to. I feel like this might be my only chance to try and make things right."

Her mother nodded. "Okay. But you must prepare yourself for the worst. If she doesn't want to see you, then you return home. I don't want you making a pest of yourself."

"I know," Mia said.

Her mother gave her a kiss and a hug and wished her luck, and then Mia walked to the car with Gail. Mia sat in the back, alone, and it felt strange, not having Lacy there next to her. Since it was Sunday morning, the roads were fairly empty, and they made good time. Mia used the miles to rehearse in her mind what she wanted to say to Lacy.

She rubbed her bracelet for luck. And then, hoping for a bit of help from her friends, she slipped the bracelet off the left wrist and moved it to the right one. Just as she expected, a camp memory came into focus. She leaned back into the leather seat and closed her eyes.

This time, she saw the four girls canoeing on the lake. Mia and Caitlin sat in the back with paddles, while Hannah and Libby sat toward the front.

"Let's pretend we're explorers, about to discover the American West," Hannah had said.

"Like Lewis and Clark, right?" Caitlin had asked. "They spent lots of time on the river, going to Oregon."

"Don't forget Sacajawea," Mia had said. "She was with them."

"Look, explorers, there's a bear!" Hannah had called out, pointing across the lake. "Over there."

Mia and Libby had both jumped out of their seats, excited about the possibility of seeing a bear. The sudden movement at both ends of the canoe had caused the boat to tip right over, dumping all four girls into the lake, screaming and laughing as they went.

Of course they all had on life preservers, so they were perfectly safe. And completely soaked.

"Where's the bear?" Mia had asked, still trying hard to see it.

Hannah had splashed water at her. "I was teasing, silly. We were pretending to be *explorers*, remember? And explorers find things."

"Well why didn't you say so?" Caitlin had asked. "It's not like we could read your mind."

"But where's the fun in that?" Hannah had said. "*Oh, girls, look, it's a pretend bear across the way.* If I had said that, none of you would have looked!"

"And we wouldn't have fallen out of the canoe either," Libby had teased.

Although they kind of gave Hannah a hard time about it, none of the girls were truly mad. In the coming days, they joked a lot about the bear.

"Hey, do you see the bear hiding behind the art easel?"

"Wait, is that the bear standing over by the cereal station? I bet he likes the Fruity O's best."

"The bear got into your underwear and is prancing around the cabin wearing some of it!"

Lying? Or pretending? What had Hannah really done?

The girls had never questioned it, when Hannah had explained that in her mind, in that particular moment, she had been pretending.

Mia knew what she had done to Lacy was much different. She had lied to her friends about her relationship with Lacy. And in the process, she'd hurt Lacy's feelings.

But there was one little thing in that memory that Mia pulled out and held on to tightly. Whether it was lying or pretending or a little bit of both, Hannah hadn't told the truth about the bear. And yet, the girls had found it in their hearts to forgive her.

Chapter 23

Mockingbird
Stops at Nothing to protect its Nest

"Hello?" Gail called out as she and Mia walked into the gigantic house. "Lacy? Are you downstairs somewhere, sweetheart?"

Gail handed Mia the envelope of photos. "They are marvelous. Do show them to Lacy, for they will surely make her feel better."

"I will," Mia replied.

Though Mia suddenly wondered if this was such a good idea. What if Lacy refused to see Mia, like her mother had suggested might happen? Could Mia really ask the driver to turn right around and take her home? How completely embarrassing.

No, Mia thought. She would make Lacy hear her out, even if she had to do it through a closed door.

Alice appeared, once again wearing her simple black dress. Mia decided it must be a uniform of sorts.

"Oh," Alice said. "Hello, Mia. I didn't know you would be paying us a visit today."

"Hi," Mia said. "I'm sorry if I shouldn't be here. I heard Lacy wasn't feeling well, and I have something I want to give her. Is she up in her room?"

"Yes, she is," Alice said. "Why don't you go on up?" She turned to Gail. "Is there anything else I can do for you?"

"Nope," Gail said. "Just helping out a friend here. Think I'll leave the two girls alone. Anything I can help you with, Alice? I'm as free as a bird today."

"Well, now that you mention it," Alice said, "I could use some help filling up the bird feeders."

Gail grinned and rubbed her hands together. "Absolutely. Perfect. That's just the job for me." She gave Mia a little wave. "See you later, and best of luck to you."

"Thanks," Mia said.

She made her way up the stairs, her bag with the photos slung over her shoulder. She counted as she went, all the way to thirty-three at the top of the staircase.

Mia took a deep breath before she turned and headed in the direction of Lacy's room. When she reached her door, she leaned in and listened to see if she could hear anything. What if she'd gone back to bed? The last thing Mia wanted to do was wake her up.

Knock, she told herself. *Just put your hand up, hit the door, and get it over with.* And yet, she couldn't. She had come here, uninvited. Lacy would be surprised. More than surprised. Shocked. What if she called security and had Mia arrested?

Wouldn't the kids at school love talking about *that* story?

Mia knew she was being ridiculous with all of these "what-ifs," and yet, her heart was beating ridiculously hard and fast. She couldn't remember the last time she'd been this nervous.

It's like a Band-Aid, she thought. *You just have to rip it off.*

Knock, knock, knock.

She waited, wondering if Lacy could hear her pounding heart from the other side of the door.

"Come in," Lacy said.

"But you don't know who it is," Mia called back. "What if it's someone you don't want to see? Do you still want me to come in?"

Lacy didn't reply for a moment.

"You can come in," she finally replied.

A step in the right direction, Mia thought.

When Mia walked into the room, she found Lacy sitting at the coffee table, photos spread out all over. She was working on her scrapbook.

"It's so weird," Lacy said. "I was *just* thinking about you. And then you knocked. It was like . . ."

"Magic?" Mia said, finishing the sentence for her.

"Yes," Lacy said. "Like magic. Now if I just had a spell to make you disappear. . . ."

Mia gulped. The words stung. She turned back toward the door, mad at herself for thinking this might work.

"Mia, I'm kidding," Lacy called out. "I'm sorry. That was mean."

"I probably deserve it," Mia said.

"Did you bring the photos from last week's birding trip?"

"Yes."

Lacy jumped up. "Ohmygosh, hurry up and get over here! I can't wait to see them."

Mia was confused. Lacy didn't seem very angry. At all. Things almost seemed normal.

As Mia hobbled toward the couch and the coffee table, she spoke quickly and without taking a single breath. "Before

I give them to you, I want you to know I'm really sorry about what I said last week. About not being your friend. The kids just got to me and I didn't know what to do. I wanted them to leave me alone. I hated that they were making fun of us, and I just wanted it to stop. I really want to be friends, and I hope you can forgive me."

With all of the words out there, Mia sank into the couch, trickles of sweat dripping down her back.

She'd done it. Mia had gotten Lacy to see her, and she'd said what she wanted to say. What happened next was up to Lacy.

Mia waited. Lacy kneeled by the coffee table and tinkered with the photos she was working on, trying them out in different places on the page.

Finally, Lacy put the photos down and looked at Mia. "It's hard being a celebrity. But I know I'm not supposed to complain about that because there are also a lot of good things about it too. The thing is, Mia, being a friend of a celebrity is probably hard too. Maybe even harder than being the celebrity, I don't know. I hadn't thought of that before we met. And I decided, after we dropped you off on Sunday, I probably shouldn't do that to you."

"So wait," Mia said, trying to understand. "You weren't really mad at me then?"

"No. I mean, I guess it hurt for a few minutes, but your voice mails and texts told me you felt bad. I figured it was just something you said to get them to knock it off."

"But you let me think that you were mad."

Lacy moved from the floor to the couch. "Yes."

"Even if that meant we might not see each other again?"

Lacy nodded. "Yes. So you could go back to your regular, drama-free life, and I could keep all the drama to myself."

"Why?"

"Because drama comes with the job. And like I said, while there is bad stuff with this job, there's also a lot of good stuff too. But as my friend, you wouldn't get any good stuff, just the bad stuff. How is that even fair?"

Mia couldn't believe what she was hearing. Lacy hadn't been upset, she'd simply been trying to protect Mia. "Of course there's good stuff!"

Lacy looked at Mia like she couldn't believe what *she* was hearing. "Like what?"

Mia threw her arms out wide. "You! Our friendship. That's the good stuff."

Tears filled Lacy's eyes. "Really?"

"Yes, really."

"I think that might be the nicest thing anybody's ever said to me," Lacy said softly.

"And by the way," Mia said, "when we go birding next time, I'm not going to take your money. Now that we're friends, it wouldn't be right. I'll find some other way to pay for camp next year."

Mia's hand flew to her mouth after the last sentence was out. She hadn't meant to say that to Lacy. She didn't want Lacy to know about her money problems.

Lacy gave her a stern look. "You have to let me pay you, then."

"No."

"Yes."

"No."

"You are so stubborn," Lacy said, trying not to smile. "Hey, can I see last week's photos now?"

Mia reached into her bag and pulled out the envelopes and handed them to Lacy. Then she said, "Oh, I almost forgot, I have one more thing." Mia took the frame out and gave it to her. "A little gift. To show you how sorry I am."

Lacy gasped as her eyes took in each of the pictures Mia had framed. "Ohmygosh, Mia. These photos are gorgeous. Your best work yet."

"You think so?" Mia asked.

"Absolutely. I can't wait to show this to Grandma." She paused. "And someone else I know too."

"Who?" Mia asked.

Lacy's eyes twinkled. "I think I'll let it be a surprise for now. You like surprises, don't you?"

"Usually," Mia replied. "Except when I fall off a stool and am surprised to find out I broke a bone. Not a fan of surprises then."

Lacy laughed. "This will be a much better surprise. I promise."

Chapter 24

Red-tailed Hawk
a good eater

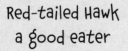

The following week, Mia got her cast off. "My foot is free! Just in time for Halloween," she told her mom as they drove to the mall after the doctor's appointment. "I can go trick-or-treating and I won't slow anyone down."

"What do you want to be this year?" she asked.

"I'm going to dress like a bird-watcher," Mia told her. "Lacy's letting me borrow her binoculars along with her grandma's hat she wears every time she goes birding. And I'll use that old canteen you kept of Dad's, and wear that too."

"Do you think people will know what you are?" her mother asked.

Mia smiled. "They will when they see the owl going trick-or-treating with me."

"An owl?" Mia's mom asked. "Who's dressing up as an owl?"

"Lacy is, and we're going to go trick-or-treating together. It's the coolest costume. She ordered it online. It has an amazing mask and when she wears it, no one will have any clue that it's her. Mom, she hasn't been trick-or-treating since she was like four years old. Can you believe that?"

"You two will have lots of fun, then," Mia's mom replied.

They pulled into the mall parking lot, and Mia felt her excitement growing. Her mom had asked Mia what she wanted to do to celebrate the cast coming off. Mia had told her she wanted to go to the mall and get a big cinnamon roll and then shop for a charm for the bracelet so she could send it on to the next girl. So that's what they did.

When they reached the jewelry counter, the saleswoman asked how she could assist them.

"Do you have any bird charms?"

"Yes," she said. "Right here."

When she saw the charm, she said, "It's perfect. I'd like to buy it, please."

"Certainly," the woman said. "Would you like me to put it on your bracelet for you, so you can wear it home?"

"Oh," Mia said, unfastening the bracelet. "Sure. That'd be great."

"It's a lovely bracelet," she told Mia as she took it and stepped away to add the new charm.

All the way home, Mia fingered the two charms, occasionally looking down and thinking how cute they looked together. Later, when she took off the bracelet, she stared at her empty wrist as she realized how much she was going to miss wearing it.

With a big sigh, she wrapped the bracelet in some tissue paper and then sat down to write a letter to go with it.

DEAR LIBBY,

SURPRISE! YOU GET THE CHARM BRACELET NEXT! I KNOW HOW HARD IT CAN BE TO WORRY ABOUT YOUR FAMILY BUSINESS, SO I FIGURED YOU COULD USE ALL THE LUCK YOU CAN GET.

DO YOU LIKE THE CHARM? BIRDS HAVE BEEN A BIG PART OF MY LIFE FOR THE PAST MONTH, SO IT SEEMED LIKE A GOOD CHOICE. IF YOU EVER GET A CHANCE TO GO BIRD-WATCHING, YOU SHOULD GO. I KNOW THAT IT SOUNDS LIKE A WEIRD THING

TO DO, BUT IT'S FUN. REALLY! THERE ARE SO MANY DIFFERENT TYPES OF BIRDS; I'M KIND OF AMAZED. SOME ARE PRETTY UGLY AND SOME ARE GORGEOUS. THERE ARE A BUNCH OF THEM THAT I'VE SEEN AND ADMIRED, BUT I THINK MY FAVORITE WOULD HAVE TO BE THE LIGHT-FOOTED CLAPPER RAIL.

HERE'S THE THING ABOUT THAT BIRD. IT CAN BE DIFFICULT TO FIND, AND WHILE WE SEARCHED AND SEARCHED, WEEK AFTER WEEK, I STARTED TO WONDER IF IT WOULD BE WORTH IT.

I KEPT TELLING MYSELF THE SEARCH IS PART OF THE FUN. AND IT WAS. BUT WHEN I FINALLY DID SEE A CLAPPER RAIL, I FELT SO THANKFUL TO HAVE SPENT JUST A LITTLE BIT OF TIME WITH IT. LIKE MY LIFE WAS BETTER BECAUSE OF THE TIME WE SPENT TOGETHER AND THE MEMORIES I NOW HAVE OF THAT SPECIAL BIRD.

IT REMINDS ME OF MY NEW FRIEND, LACY BELL. (EVERYTHING IS FINE WITH HER, BY THE WAY. I APOLOGIZED, SHE FORGAVE ME, AND WE'RE GOOD.) I WASN'T SURE AT FIRST HOW THINGS WOULD TURN OUT WITH HER, BUT NOW, MY LIFE IS BETTER BECAUSE OF THE TIME WE'VE SPENT TOGETHER.

SOMETIMES IT CAN BE HARD OR SCARY SEARCHING FOR A

GOOD FRIEND. BUT THE CLAPPER RAIL WILL ALWAYS REMIND
ME THAT IT'S WORTH THE TROUBLE IN THE END.

NEXT WEEK, AFTER HALLOWEEN IS OVER AND OUT OF
THE WAY, LACY IS PICKING ME UP FOR A SPECIAL SURPRISE.
I HAVE NO IDEA WHAT IT IS, BUT I'M DYING TO KNOW.

MY LAST PIECE OF NEWS IS THAT MY CAST CAME OFF
TODAY. HOORAY!!!! I CAN'T WAIT TO GO SURFING ONE
DAY SOON.

I MISS YOU, LIBBY. HAVE FUN WEARING THE BRACELET.
I WISH I COULD MAIL MYSELF ALONG WITH THE
BRACELET. INSTEAD, I'LL JUST HAVE TO WAIT AND SEE YOU
AT CAMP NEXT SUMMER. IF WE'RE ALL BACK AT CAMP
AGAIN NEXT YEAR. I HOPE WITH ALL OF MY HEART THAT
WE ARE.

YOUR CABIN 7 BFF,
MIA

There was a knock on the door. Lacy got up and answered
it. Josie and Salina stood there, dressed in their wetsuits,
holding their surfboards.

"Well. What are you waiting for?" Salina asked.

"You guys," Mia said with a smile. "This is really

sweet of you, but I still have to take it kind of easy. No surfing for a few more weeks." She looked at the clock. "Did you even look at the time? It'll be dark soon anyway."

Both Josie and Salina groaned. "We were just so excited for you," Josie said.

"We need to figure out something else we can do then. To celebrate," Salina said.

"I know," Josie said. "Let's go out for pigs in a bunk bed. The restaurant serves breakfast all day."

"And I'm happy to drive you girls there," Mia's mom said.

"Sounds perfect," Mia said as she pulled out her phone. "But on one condition. We invite a friend of mine to come along."

The girls' eyes got big. "You mean, you're going to ask Lacy to come with us?" Josie asked.

"I promise you'll like her," Mia said. "And there's no better time to meet her than over plates of pigs in a bunk bed. She's probably never even heard of them before."

"Seriously?" Salina said. "But that's so sad."

"I know, right?" Mia said. "You two go home and change and come back here when you're ready to go."

Salina and Josie said good-bye just as Lacy answered the phone. Mia invited Lacy along to join them for dinner. Well, breakfast for dinner.

"I'd love to, but what if the paparazzi follow me there? It could get pretty annoying, them taking pictures of us all night long."

"It's okay," Mia told her. "We can handle it. Lacy, you can't be like the clapper rail. You can't hide forever. You're missing out on too much. If they want to take pictures of four girls chatting and eating, so what? Unless you're ashamed of me or something."

"Mia," Lacy said. "You are the best. How could I ever be ashamed of you?"

"What if I told you we're having pigs in a bunk bed for dinner?"

Lacy laughed. "Um. What is that, exactly?"

"Layers of pancakes with sausages tucked in between," Mia explained.

"Oh," Lacy said. "That sounds good. Nothing to be ashamed of at all." She paused. "Unless you're going to dump ketchup all over the thing, like that kid you told me about. Cesar somebody. Now *that* would be shameful."

Mia laughed. "No ketchup, I promise. Just really good pancakes. And friends."

"That sounds like an awesome night to me," Lacy said.

And that's exactly what it was.

Chapter 25

Rainbow Finch
what a cutie

$\mathcal{I}$t was the day of Mia's surprise, a Saturday.

Mia stood in front of the mirror in the guest room at Lacy's house. She twirled around and around, admiring the dress she wore. Apparently wherever they were going was kind of fancy, but Lacy hadn't wanted Mia to stress over what to wear.

"I have tons of dresses and outfits and I'm sure we can find something you'll love," she'd told Mia as they made plans for the day.

Mia had picked out a simple blue dress with three-quarter-length sleeves and a skirt that flared out. She wore black tights and simple black flats she'd brought from home.

When she walked out into the hallway, Lacy was waiting for her.

"Wow," Lacy said. "You look amazing. Fabulous. Incredible!"

Mia smiled. "You sound like your grandma Gail."

"But it's all true."

"You look pretty good yourself," Mia said. Lacy wore a gorgeous antique white lace dress with red heels that matched her red lipstick. She couldn't have looked more like a movie star.

"When are you going to tell me where we're going?" Mia asked.

"Never."

"Never?"

"Nope. It will ruin the fun of the surprise. You'll see when we get there." Lacy grabbed Mia's hand and tugged at her. "Come on. The driver's waiting."

As they descended the stairs, a well-dressed woman, who had been talking to Alice near the bottom of the stairs, turned and waved. "Oh my goodness," she called out, "don't you two look like you've just stepped out of a magazine?"

"Thanks," Lacy replied. When they reached the two women, Lacy said, "Mom, this is my friend Mia."

Lacy's mom extended her hand. "So lovely to meet you, Mia."

Mia smiled and took her hand. "Thanks. You too."

"I wish I could go with you girls," Lacy's mom said, "but I have plans this evening. In fact, I need to go and get ready myself. You'll be all right, won't you, love?"

"We'll be fine," Lacy said. "Have fun."

"You too." She kissed Lacy on the cheek and then headed up the stairs.

Mia turned to Alice. "I left my camera bag by the door. Is it still there?"

"I believe so," Alice said.

"I was wondering if you'd mind taking a picture of the two of us. It's so sad that I don't have any of the two of us together."

"Of course," Alice said. "Just show me what to do, and I'm happy to do that for you."

Mia got her camera, gave Alice a quick lesson, and then Lacy and Mia posed at the bottom of the pretty staircase.

"Thanks so much," Mia said.

"You're welcome," Alice said. "Now you girls better get going. Have fun."

"We will," Lacy said.

All week Mia had tried to figure out what the

surprise could be. She knew it had something to do with her photos. She wondered if maybe Lacy had entered her in some kind of photography contest. It was the only thing she could think of that made any sense. But why did they have to dress up and go somewhere? Unless . . . Maybe the prizes were being awarded tonight at an awards ceremony.

Had Mia won something? If so, what could it be? Money? A trip? A new camera?

"I can't stand the suspense," Mia said. "I wish you'd tell me where we're going."

Lacy gave a little shrug. "I know. Sorry."

As the driver made his way down the road in the town car, Mia turned and watched the cars of paparazzi behind them. It had to get annoying having people follow you every time you left your house.

"They're always hoping they'll catch me doing something scandalous," Lacy said. "I love disappointing them all the time."

"Yeah, they seemed pretty upset that you met three boring girls for dinner a couple of weeks ago instead of meeting up with some cute boy or something," Mia said.

"I had so much fun that night at the restaurant with you and your friends," Lacy said. "I'm glad you made me come."

"Me too," Mia said.

When they reached their destination, Lacy squeezed Mia's hand. "I really hope you like your surprise."

By then, Mia was a bundle of nerves, as excitement had turned into anxiousness somewhere along the way. "Me too," Mia said truthfully.

After the driver opened the door, the girls stepped out onto the sidewalk in front of a cool modern building. Before Mia could inspect her surroundings further, a couple of large men hurried them in through the front door as camera flashes went off all around them.

"It's a private party," she heard one of them saying to someone.

A party? What kind of party?

Once inside, what Mia saw took her breath away. It was ten times better than any kind of awards event or anything else she could have imagined.

She grabbed on to Lacy's arm to steady herself as she took it all in. On a large sign to their right, printed in a beautiful font, it said, PHOTOGRAPHY BY LOCAL ARTIST MIA CRUZ.

And all around, hung on the walls, were framed prints of her photos, in various sizes.

Photos of birds, like the white pelicans, the belted king-fisher, and the light-footed clapper rail.

Photos of the shoreline at the lagoon.

Photos of various flowers and plants.

But what really amazed Mia was the fact that the room was full of people. People who were walking around the room, looking at her photos. Talking about them. And by the looks of a cash register at the back of the room, buying them as well.

"Lacy," Mia said, finally finding her voice. "What have you done?"

"Isn't it just so cool?" Lacy said, her eyes sparkling. "I called in a favor with the person who owns this gallery. He helped me get everything ready for tonight."

"But the photos," Mia said. "I only gave you prints. You didn't have the memory cards, did you?"

Lacy rubbed her hands together. "Your mom helped me with that. I stopped in at the café one day while you were at school. I had her replace the ones in your camera bag with new cards, so I could use them for the show. Pretty sneaky, right? Anyway, the gallery owner and I both spread the word to people we work with. And so, here we are."

"Wait. Are these people here because they feel sorry for me, then?" Mia asked. "I mean, what did you tell them, exactly?"

"No, they aren't here because they feel sorry for you! I told them I had a very talented friend who would be having an art show featuring her fabulous photography, and they should come and check it out. That's it. That's all they needed to know. Because it's the truth."

"I can't believe you did this," Mia said, reaching over and giving Lacy a hug. "Thank you."

"You're welcome."

Mia's eyes scanned the room, and her hand flew to her mouth when she realized Lacy wasn't the only famous person in attendance.

Mia leaned in and whispered, "Lacy, over there in the corner. The guy in the black jeans and the button-down steel-gray shirt. Is that —"

Lacy grinned. "Yep. The one and only Levi Vincent. You want to meet him? Not only is he super-cute, but he's sweet as candy too."

Mia could hardly believe this was happening. "What?

No, I can't meet him. He's my absolute favorite, and I have no idea what I would possibly say to Levi Vincent."

"Just say hi and that you're a fan of his work. But don't drool on him, okay? And hey, you could get your picture taken with him. Make all of your friends jealous." Before Mia could respond, Lacy pointed in his direction. "Look! Ohmygosh, he's buying one of the kingfisher prints. Come on, now you definitely have to meet him, since he's obviously a fan of *your* work."

"Wait," Mia said, holding Lacy back. "I'm not ready. I mean, this is not what I expected. At all." She shook her head a little, still trying to take it all in. "I know I already said it, but thank you so much for doing this. It really means a lot."

Lacy waved her hand and said, "It's not a problem. By the way, you've already sold three large prints, to my grandma. It's really adorable how excited she is about them. Now she can say good morning to her beloved clapper rail every day when she wakes up in the morning and good night before she falls asleep."

People were buying Mia's photos. Which meant Mia would get money for camp. It all seemed too good to be true.

"And to think that none of this would have happened if you hadn't come into the café that Sunday morning," Mia said.

"Right place, right time, as my grandma likes to say."

"For sure."

Lacy pulled on Mia's hand. "And you know, you are going to be so upset with yourself if you don't take advantage of this moment, right here, right now, and meet Levi Vincent."

"Do you promise you'll stay with me the entire time?" Mia asked, smoothing down her dress as they walked.

"I promise."

"Do you promise he won't think I'm weird, taking photos of different kinds of birds?"

"Weird?" Lacy said. "Why would he think that's weird?" They walked a few more steps until they were standing directly behind Levi. "Birds are awesome. Everyone knows that. Right, Levi?"

Levi turned around and gave the girls his million-dollar smile, complete with dimples. "Oh yeah. Totally awesome," he said.

Mia's favorite word, spoken by her favorite singer/actor who was buying one of her favorite photos so she could return to her favorite place next summer — Camp Brookridge.

She remembered Caitlin's words. *Sometimes awesome shows up when you least expect it.* And sometimes, Mia thought, it even shows up wearing gold sunglasses and designer shoes.

Right place. Right time. What luck!

Turn the page for a sneak peek
at Libby's *Charmed Life*!

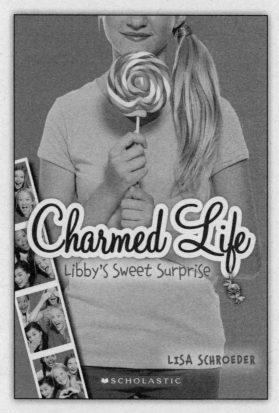

Chapter 1

Swirly whirly Lollipop
a favorite through the years

Libby climbed the stepladder and reached for the jar of chocolate frogs. *Rebecca's favorite*, she thought. They weren't real frogs, of course — white chocolate in the shape of a frog, with green coloring. A strange candy, to be sure.

Also strange? How much her best friend, Rebecca, had changed over the course of six weeks, while Libby had been away at summer camp. Try as she might, Libby couldn't figure out what had happened while she'd been away. It was as much of a mystery to her as why someone would want to eat a piece of candy in the shape of a frog.

With the jar in hand, she carefully climbed back down and went to the counter. This was her job every Saturday — to fill the jars of candy in her aunt and uncle's sweetshop. Her uncle paid her an allowance for doing so, though Libby didn't really have a choice in the matter. It was a family business, and as part of the family, she had to do her part.

When she'd begun working at the (*very* part-time) job at the age of ten, Rebecca had been so envious. "Think of how many sweets you can eat," she'd said. "After all, you must sample one of everything to make sure you don't have a bad batch."

"You're joking, right?" Libby had said. "My uncle would be so upset if I ate that many. And even if he didn't mind, just think of the stomachache I'd get."

"But it would be the sweetest stomachache of your life," Rebecca had said.

Now Libby sighed as she put the jar back where it belonged. She couldn't deny it; she missed her bestie. But Rebecca seemed to be quite taken with her new group of friends, especially the ones who were boys.

The bell over the door jingled, as it always did when a customer walked in. With the jar in its rightful place, Libby returned to the counter as her uncle rushed out from the back room to offer assistance. Except it wasn't someone looking to buy candy. It was someone delivering flowers.

"Good afternoon," the delivery man said.

"Hello," Uncle Oliver replied as he ran his hand through his messy brown hair. "More flowers, I see."

"Yes." The delivery man handed Uncle Oliver the bouquet of red and white roses before he said, "I hope you enjoy them."

"Thank you," Uncle Oliver replied.

Libby's great-grandmother had passed away the week before. Many of the townsfolk in Tunbridge Wells, England knew Libby's family because of the candy store they owned: Mr. Pemberton's Olde Sweetshop. It was nice that people were thinking of them, Libby thought, but their house was beginning to look too much like a floral shop. Every day her uncle brought the flowers home, since there wasn't room for them in their small place of business.

"I hope this is the last of them," Uncle Oliver said. "Is that terrible of me to say?"

"No, because I was thinking the same thing," Libby said.

Her uncle smiled. "It's very thoughtful of everyone. And kind. And we appreciate it, of course."

"Yes," Libby said. "Too bad people don't send something a little more useful, though."

"When your parents died all those years ago," he said as he set the bouquet down in a spot next to the register, "and you came to live with us, friends and acquaintances brought us meals. It was quite nice, although we didn't have much of an appetite for a time afterwards."

Libby didn't remember much from that time, since she'd been so young. "I know what you mean," she replied, walking out from behind the counter. "It's hard to eat when you're sad. The last morning at Camp Brookridge, before we all had to head for home, hardly anyone ate their breakfast."

The bell above the door jingled again, and this time, much to their relief, some customers strolled in. As Uncle Oliver walked over to greet the Thomason family, Libby started to sneak out, through the back. Her duties were done, and she was ready to go home. Libby and her uncle had an agreement that once the jars had been restocked, Libby could leave. But she heard Mrs. Thomason say something that made her stop and listen.

"Are you worried about the new sweetshop opening up soon?" Mrs. Thomason was asking her uncle.

"Not worried at all," Uncle Oliver replied with a smile. "As you know, this shop has been in my family for fifty years, and no one knows sweets like we do. I am certain we will always have the best selection in town. Now, what may I help you with today?"

As he turned, he spotted Libby, and so she waved to let him know she was heading for home. Once outside, she hopped on her bike and pedaled, thinking about what her uncle had said.

Not worried at all.

She knew, from conversations her aunt and uncle had at home, that wasn't exactly true. Having another sweetshop fairly close by was pretty worrisome. Candy wasn't like produce; a person could go months without eating any. And now that there would be two shops in town, it could mean half the amount of business for the Pembertons.

Thankfully, their somewhat small town, which was quaint and charming and a wonderful place to live, did get a fair number of tourists every year. After all, there was much to see and do, with beautiful gardens and a few castles in the area to explore. People also came to visit the well-known Chalybeate Spring, discovered some four hundred years ago and, at one time, believed to miraculously cure people's illnesses.

But even with the tourists, it was hard to imagine that two sweetshops could really thrive in a town that wasn't especially large.

Libby recalled the time she'd tried to describe her English town to her three camp BFFs, Mia, Caitlin, and Hannah. They'd all been so curious about what it was like for Libby to live in England, since none of them had ever traveled outside of the States.

"It's quite lovely," she'd told them. "We're not very far from London, maybe sixty kilometers or so, and we're surrounded by gorgeous countryside. My uncle says we're fortunate to have some of England's best gardens near by."

"What are the houses like?" Caitlin had asked Libby.

"We have many large, Victorian houses, but there are also lots of clapboard cottages too," Libby had said.

"I'm not really sure what any of that means," Mia had said, "but it sounds awesome!"

"The three of us should visit her one day," Hannah had said. "Wouldn't that be something, all of us in jolly old England?"

They'd all agreed it would be a lot of fun.

It only took Libby a few minutes to get home. When she walked in the front door, the smell of freshly baked bread greeted her. Her aunt yelled, "Hi, Libby. I'm in the kitchen. Come see what the postman brought for you."

She couldn't get to the kitchen fast enough. Her aunt Jayne stood there wearing a cute green-and-blue apron, her curly brown hair pulled back with barrettes, as she held the package out in front of her. Libby clapped her hands together quickly before she grabbed it and read the name of the person who sent it.

"It's from Mia!" Libby cried, and took off for her room, her long ponytail swishing side to side as went. "I'd hoped it would be something from one of my summer camp friends."

"Everything go all right at the shop today?" her aunt called after her.

Libby stopped and turned around. "Yes. We got more flowers."

"Brilliant," Aunt Jayne said. "Just what we need. All right, go along and open your package. I can't wait to see what it is, when you feel like sharing."

"I can't wait either," Libby whispered as she closed her door.

Confectionately Yours

Don't miss all the books in this delicious series!

Four girls, one charm bracelet, and a little bit of luck . . .

Charmed Life
Caitlin's Lucky Charm

LISA SCHROEDER

SCHOLASTIC

Charmed Life
Mia's Golden Bird

LISA SCHROEDER

SCHOLASTIC

Charmed Life
Libby's Sweet Surprise

LISA SCHROEDER

SCHOLASTIC

Charmed Life
Hannah's Bright Star

LISA SCHROEDER

SCHOLASTIC

From the author of *It's Raining Cupcakes* comes a charming series about how anything is possible when you have great friends!